Barbara Bontrager

Mari's Mountain

Mari's Mountain

Dorothy Hamilton

Illustrated by Esther Rose Graber

HERALD PRESS
Scottdale, Pennsylvania
Kitchener, Ontario
1978

Library of Congress Cataloging in Publication Data

Hamilton, Dorothy, 1906-
 Mari's mountain.

 SUMMARY: Abused by her alcoholic father, Mari runs
away from home to build a new life for herself in a big
city.
 [1. Runaways—Fiction] 1. Graber, Esther Rose.
II. Title.
PZ7.H18136Mar   [Fic]   78-10620
ISBN 0-8361-1868-5
ISBN 0-8361-1869-3 pbk.

MARI'S MOUNTAIN
Copyright © 1978 by Herald Press, Scottdale, Pa., 15683
 Published simultaneously in Canada by Herald Press,
 Kitchener, Ont. N2G 4M5
Library of Congress Catalog Card Number: 78-10620
International Standard Book Numbers:
 0-8361-1868-5 (hardcover)
 0-8361-1869-3 (softcover)
Printed in the United States of America
Design: Alice B. Shetler

10 9 8 7 6 5 4 3 2 1

To
Dolph Briscoe
because of his concern for runaways

Chapter 1

Mari upended her denim shoulder bag, and the contents spilled onto the yellow spread. A package of Lifesavers rolled to the edge before lodging in the bumpy chenille. *I forgot about stuffing them in there when I decided I couldn't stand living at home one more day. Wonder what else is in here, and how much money I have left.*

She picked up the snap coin purse and the crocheted envelope which she'd used for a billfold when she had any paper money. *Seven dollars! Is that all I have left of the twenty I snitched from Mom? I kind of hated to take it from her. But Dad*

*keeps a grab on his money and after all she's work-
ing now.*

As Mari counted the coins she decided she should
have hitchhiked to the city. *That bus ticket took
over four dollars and I had to pay a week ahead for
this room. But I'm not brave enough to get out and
catch rides. Running away is about all I can
manage now. But I'm still not sorry I left.*

*There's more change than I thought. I'm glad I
remembered to empty my dime bank. It's a wonder
there was anything left the way I kept robbing it.
Thirty dimes plus the other change—that's four
dollars and forty-six cents.*

She left the roll of candy mints and the half
package of cheese crackers on the bed and stuffed
the money, the blue hair curlers, the comb, the wad
of Kleenex, the pack and a half of cigarettes, and
the black and white head scarf back in the bag,
making sure the money was at the bottom. The last
article was the bluebird music box her mother had
given her for her eleventh birthday. *It's a wonder it
works as many times as I've wound it up.* She
pulled away the facial tissue wrapping and turned
the metal disk. As she set the ceramic bird on the
end table it began to circle and she listened to a
tinkling version of the song "Sunrise, Sunset." *It's
sort of sad,* she thought, *but still it's pretty. I'm
glad I brought it along, and glad it didn't break.*

Mari looked around the room. *It's not so bad. Better than mine at home, really,* she thought. The
three-cornered tear in the tan window blind was up
high enough so that no one could peep through it
and the one chair was a rocker with an orange

cushion. *I can be comfortable in it. But what can I do when I sit? No television, no—oh, I'm glad I put my transistor in my suitcase.*

As she hurried to open the dented luggage she remembered the woman had said when she'd asked if she could rent a room. "I reckon I can take a chance on you. You got luggage, not just one of them bags slung over your shoulder. I don't rent to drifters." Then she looked straight into Mari's face and said, "If you can pay, you can stay."

As she flipped the catch on the gray plastic suitcase Mari thought, *I was sure she was going to ask how old I am. Maybe it was good I happened to hear what a girl said at the Candy Box last week. I guess I was getting ready to split then.*

The girl had been in the next booth and Mari listened as she sipped a chocolate malt, jabbing the chunk of ice cream with the straw, wishing it was her dad. *I can't stand the way he yelled at me when I got home from school, not because of what I'd done but on account of what he'd drunk.*

"There are tricks," another girl said. "Like ways to get a place to stay."

"Where do you stay?" someone else asked.

"Well, me, I'm choosy. I don't shack up 'less there's no other way. If I've got bread and want to spend it for a bed I try to look older. These landladies are scared to take in kids. We're too risky, they think." The girl whose face Mari didn't see told how she either tucked her long hair under a scarf or put it in braids and wound one over each ear. "That's kind of old-fashioned, but it fools people. I always carry big wire hairpins."

9

I didn't do that because my hair's not that long, Mari thought. *But the lady didn't ask me how old I am. I wonder why?*

She decided to unpack. *I know I'll be here a week. I've paid for that. 'Less Dad catches up with me.* She hung her extra pair of jeans and the two dresses she'd brought in the closet. The girl in the booth had said that it was a good idea to take dresses. "If you want to make it on your own, and get a straight job, you'll have to wear something besides jeans and sandals." *It's a good thing I have new loafers in case anyone hires me.* Then a new problem came to her. *Do you have to have a permit or something to get a job?* she wondered. She shook her head. *I don't want to think about what I'll do when the money runs out. Besides, I'm hungry.*

She scrubbed her face in the half bath, reminding herself to look for the bathroom that was somewhere down the hall. *I'd like to go to that hamburger place I saw on the way from the bus station. I think I will! Then maybe I can slip some food in my room. Cheaper stuff.*

It was still daylight whan Mari left the house. *That's good. I'd feel a little scared on the streets of a strange city after dark. Sometimes I was even afraid back in Castleton at night. Even when I argued with Dad that I was old enough to be out late.*

She went to the long counter after standing back and studying the menu on the back wall. "I'd like two cheeseburgers and hot chocolate, please."

"To go?"

"No. For here."

Mari took the brown plastic tray to a table in the corner of the room, walking slowly to avoid sloshing the hot chocolate over the rim of the brown cup. *Those french fries look real good,* she thought, *but two cheeseburgers don't cost much more and they'll fill me up better.*

As she unwrapped a sandwich she looked out the windows. Cars rolled past until the line was stopped by a red light up the street. *There are sure a lot of people in this big city,* she thought. *And I don't know the name of a single one of them.*

She took her time eating, not being in a hurry to get back to the strange room. The cheeseburgers were hot and she enjoyed each bite. She noticed for the first time that some customers stopped at a salad bar between the counter and eating sections. *Is that for me too, or does it cost extra?* She was tempted to help herself but decided she should ask. *It wouldn't help to get myself arrested the first day I'm a runaway.*

A lady was helping a little boy put catsup on french fries at the next table. "Excuse me, please," Mari asked. "Are we supposed to help ourselves to lettuce and stuff?"

"Yes. If you didn't have it put on at the counter."

"Thank you."

As she lifted curls of lettuce and two tomato slices to a paper plate with tongs, Mari thought, *I'd better not be a pig just because it's here.* She watched the little boy as she finished her meal. He turned the chair that went only so far then he swung it back the other way. *That must be his grandma,* she thought. *She's not making him* hurry. *She just keeps saying, "Isn't it time you took another bite, Craig?" Mothers have to be in more of a hurry, I guess. Anyway, Mom always was.*

For the first time that day Mari thought about how her mother would feel when she didn't come home. *Of course she won't know it until she gets off work at the motel. And maybe she won't even look in my room right away. I suppose she'll worry when she realizes I ran off. But I don't want to think about that now.*

As soon as Mari walked out the door she fastened the top snap on her denim jacket. The wind was blowing harder. A yellow wrapper from a cheeseburger fluttered across the parking lot and the orange and red sign in front of the drive-in swung back and forth. By the time she reached the brown shingled house a few raindrops had spotted the sidewalk. As she walked up the four concrete steps she noticed that the "Room for rent" sign was gone from the front window. *I guess that means I got here just in time or else there wouldn't have been a place for me here.*

The smell of food came from the back of the house and water was running. *She's cooking meat and something else, cabbage maybe. I wonder what the woman's name is. She didn't say. She didn't even ask mine. Why?*

Mari heard music from behind one door, but no sound from any of the other rooms. *How many people stay here,* she wondered as she tiptoed down the hall to find the bathroom. *There can't be more than four, unless two stay together. That's all the rooms there are.* She wondered why she was being

12

quiet. *What difference does it make if they see me? I don't know them and they don't know me.*

She felt safer when she turned the key in the lock. After hanging her jacket over a chair to dry, she picked up her transistor and walked to the window. She turned the plastic dial as she looked out the window. Rain was streaming down the screen wire, making the squares into little windows. *I'm glad I'm not hitchhiking out there,* she thought. Music blared from a station. She turned the volume down and was ready to tune in to some livelier music when she heard the words, "I'd climb the highest mountain."

She kicked her blue sneakers off as she went to the bed and lay down. *I'll find out if anyone's using that tub or shower or whatever later.* She rested her head on the palm of her hand and as she shut her eyes she thought, *Who'd want to climb a mountain anyway—for anyone? Seems kind of dumb to me.*

Chapter 2

The room was dark except for a dim glow from a streetlight when Mari opened her eyes. She raised her head, not sure for a minute where she was. Had her mother moved the bed so the light came from a different direction? Then she realized. *I'm not home.*

She felt thirsty and stumbled to the half bath and flipped the light switch on. Seven paper cups were stacked upside down on a narrow shelf above the sink. *That Mrs. Whatever-her-name-is doesn't believe in wasting anything. One paper cup a day for the week.* Mari let the water run until the red rustiness in it washed away. *Looks like no one's used this room for a while.*

She had no idea how long she'd slept until she turned her radio on. *Two o'clock. Not near time to get up.* She lay awake thinking about tomorrow. *What will I do? Look for a job? Will they ask me my age? I can't live long on the money that's left.*

Then a feeling of fear, a kind of chill, made her pull the thin blanket over her head. What would happen when she didn't show up at school? She knew that the attendance clerk checked on whether kids were really sick. They did that to her twice. *Once it was okay because I had tonsillitis.* The other time she'd skipped school and went out to the mall with Sally Deane, who spent more time hanging around there than she did at school.

As Mari remembered that day, a little more than a month before, she thought, *It really wasn't that much fun. I don't see why Sally gets such a kick out of skipping school, and it certainly wasn't worth the belt-whipping Dad gave me. That was the day I began to think of running away sometime. I vowed I'd never stand still for another beating. Then I began to talk about it to Lois Ann and some others.*

The next time Mari opened her eyes she was hungry instead of thirsty. *I'd better see if anyone's using the tub and get something to eat,* she decided. Later, as she dressed she ate two of the cheese crackers. *I ought to get some more of this snack stuff at a grocery someplace.*

She wore her black-and-white-checked dress with the wide collar and cuffs. *It might be better for job hunting than the pink one, on account of the lace.*

15

As she walked down the stairs she saw the woman who'd rented her the room. "Morning," Mari mumbled.

"Morning," the lady said. She looked up from the tall fern she was watering with a long-spouted can.

"That's a real fine fern," Mari said.

"Yes. It's doing real good. Before you go, did I mention that I have the room cleaned just once a week? In case you're staying."

"Yes'm. I'm aiming to. And it's okay about the cleaning. I'm used to picking up after myself."

"Most folks don't. You'd never believe the messes I've seen. At the moment I've got a pretty good class of roomers."

I must remember that, Mari thought. *If I'm careful about my room maybe it'll help in case I don't have rent money.*

"Well, I ought to be on the way," Mari said. "But, I'd like to know your name."

"Didn't I say? It's Lou Cardmon. Lou's short for Louise."

"I like Louise best."

"So do I. But no one calls me that anymore."

That's another thing I'll do. I'll call her Louise. Maybe that's a little sneaky—kind of buttering her up. But that's what she said she liked.

Mari passed the Jiffy Market she'd seen the day before. *I can get some snacks there as long as I have some money. What I need now is a diner, or a doughnut and coffee shop.* She had decided to stop at a drugstore and see if there was a lunch counter when she saw a familiar sign up the street and over one block. *That's like the motel where Mom works.*

16

It must be part of the same chain. She changed her mind about stopping at the drugstore. Instead she headed toward the blinking lights.

She knew enough about motels to realize it would be better not to ask the desk clerk about a job. *He doesn't have anything to do with hiring people.* She walked through the lobby and into the dining room. Not more than seven people were eating at the square tables. The faces of two were hidden by opened newspapers. A girl in a tan uniform with a cream apron came through the swinging half-doors at the back. Mari hurried to the cash register and asked, "Who would I see about a job?"

"Ellie," the girl said. "She's not in yet."

"A *woman* manages the motel?"

"No. Just this dining room. It's kind of separate from the rest of the business."

"Well, thanks. Will Ellie be in by the time I finish eating?"

"Sure, if you don't eat too fast. Take a seat. I'll be with you in a minute. Here, might as well take a menu along and save me a step or two."

Mari decided on a small order of pancakes and milk. As she ate she watched the people who came in and out of the swinging doors. *They seem to get along okay. They joke and laugh a lot together.*

"Are you the girl who's interested in a job?" someone asked as Mari sipped her milk. She turned and looked into the face of a tall lady who wore silver-rimmed glasses.

"Yes. I'm Mari Clayton."

"Have you had any experience?"

"Some. I worked in a cafeteria where I lived

17

before." She didn't see any need to mention that it was the school cafeteria. "And my mother worked in a motel for a long time. I've been around one a lot."

"Well, if you're not particular about what you do, I can give you a chance, on a part-time basis. An hour and a half at noon and the same at night."

"That would be fine," Mari said. "When would I start?"

"The sooner, the better. A girl quit last night because she found fulltime work. Here, give me that check. You get two meals here, with a dollar and a half limit on each. Or would you rather eat free later?"

"No. Now's fine," Mari said. She wanted to ask how much she'd be paid and when. *But anything's better than nothing. I never thought I'd be this lucky. To get a job first try.*

"One more thing," Ellie said. "You have a Social Security number, I suppose."

For a minute Mari's heart seemed to stop. *I had one, but I don't remember seeing it when I dumped the stuff out of my bag.* Then she reached for the knit envelope that was her billfold. "It's in here, I think. Behind the lining."

As the manager looked at the card she said, "Marian. Didn't you say Mary?"

"Yes'm. Mari, with 'i' on the end. It's kind of a nickname."

"I see. Well, you come back to the kitchen when you've finished. To meet the others and look around."

Mari took a deep breath as she moved the last

piece of pancake back and forth in the buttery syrup. *I was scared she was going to ask how old I am. I wonder why she didn't? Do I look older? Or did she think if I wasn't out of school I'd be there?*

Then she remembered how her dad had yelled when he heard about her getting the Social Security number. "More of this women's lib malarkey," he said.

"It's because of taking driver's training," Mari's mother explained. "She has to have it."

"More malarkey. She'll never get her hands on my steering wheel."

Mari shook her head. *I don't want to remember what else he said. The drunker he is, the worse he talks, all those rotten words. His whiskey-talk stinks. Anyway, it's lucky I had to get this card.*

The girl who'd taken Mari's order came to the table. "Ellie says you'll be a part-timer. I'm Liz. You're Mari?"

"Right!"

"You'll be okay here if you do what Ellie expects. She's strict about giving good service and keeping things clean and not mixing it up with the customers. But she's fair."

"You been here long?"

"For five years—except when my little boy was born. I took a seven-week vacation three years ago, if that's what you can call it."

Mari wanted to say that Liz didn't look old enough to have a son three years old. *But it's not too smart to go to talking about age. Not for me anyhow.*

19

Chapter 3

The manager was sliding a pan of sweet rolls out of the oven when Mari went through the swinging doors. She smiled and said, "I'll be with you in a minute. As soon as I get these into the bun warmer."

"Do you bake your own rolls?"

"No, but I like to heat them through. About you working here, I should have told you what I had in mind. The only job open right now is running the dishwasher."

Mari felt relieved. She'd been a little uneasy. She had cooked some at home, more than any of the girls she knew, because her mother went to work at the motel. But she knew she wouldn't be good at a lot of things. "That's all right," she said. "I've run one before."

Ellie Straley turned the switch of the square Monel Metal appliance and ran a partly filled tray of dishes through to show Mari how it worked. "When they come out on the other side, stack them here," she said. "They'll be hot."

"I know. What hours shall I plan to work?"

"From twelve to one-thirty. The few dishes and silver we need before and after that we can manage. And one more thing. Uniforms are furnished—like the ones the other girls are wearing."

She still didn't say how much they'll pay me. But I'll find out. And getting two meals a day will really be great. I think I'll eat the next one tonight.

As she walked through the lobby, Mari looked at the brown clock which was either made of plastic or real wood. *Ten o'clock. I'll need to be back in two hours. Keeping track of time's not easy when you don't have a watch. I'm used to Mom calling me either at home or from work. A lot of things I always took for granted are up to me now.*

On the way back to her rented room she wondered whether she was supposed to wear hose on the job. *I only brought one pair. That's all I have and I stopped a run in them with nail polish. They'll have to do until I find out when I get paid. Figuring out what to buy when you're almost broke isn't easy.*

She stopped at the Jiffy Market and used five of

her dimes and a quarter to buy three oranges, a package of Twinkies, and a can of Coke from the machine. *This way I'll have something at night.* She stopped at the magazine rack and reached for a movie magazine. *No. I'd better not.*

The sun was warm and Mari sat down on the top step when she came to Louise's house. *This might have been a real nice part of town years ago,* she thought. *If the houses were painted they'd still look pretty decent.*

As she started toward the stairs she noticed that a television set was on in the room at the left of the hall. *It sure would be nice to watch a good program again. I miss TV a lot. Dad didn't let us watch when he was mean from drinking, but he wasn't always around. Things were better when Dad wasn't home. Mom laughed more and talked a lot.*

Mari pulled the orange-padded rocker to a place near the window after she'd put the snacks in a dresser drawer. *If I keep things neat a little at a time there'll be no big messes for Louise to see.*

As she watched cars pass the house she remembered a time when her father was away. He'd said he was going to look for a job that suited him. He never kept a job long. He was always quitting one job to look for a better one. *I think he was fired from some of them because he drank too much.*

Mari remembered that she and her mother had been alone for nearly a week once. *That was about the best time we ever had. Dad only left us a little money, but Mom had a few ironings to do.* She had gone to the library and had checked out some books she liked and some from a list her mother made.

Then, they took turns reading and ironing. She did the pillow slips and lunch cloths. Her mom was better at dresses and shirts.

They used money from the ironings to do what her mother called splurging. They went to the fried chicken place once and to McDonald's for cheeseburgers twice. They watched television together.

Mom was happier than I ever remember, before or after, Mari thought. *She told me stories about how it was when she was little and lived on a farm. The part I liked best was about when they were snowed in and made snow ice cream and dug caves under the drifts. She said her mom might have been worried about running out of food but she and her brother didn't. Then as soon as Dad got back she was quiet again and almost never stood up to him. Maybe if she had I wouldn't have—but there's no use thinking about that now.*

She checked on the time by listening to the transistor radio. *Guess I might as well head on back to the motel. I can wait in the lobby until noon. Maybe they'll have a magazine in the lobby.* She brushed her hair and straightened her hose, being careful not to break the seal of the nail polish and start the run again.

"Going out?" Louise said from the room where the TV was going.

"Yes, I got a part-time job. I'll be over at the motel noons and evenings."

"Then you may be staying more than a week?"

"Yes'm. It's close to the job and quiet."

"Too quiet maybe—for a young person."

Is she trying to find out how old I am? Mari

23

thought. "No. It's not bothering me."

"Well if you want to watch TV now and then you're welcome."

"Do the others?"

"No. They have their own sets," Louise said. "Didn't you hear any of them?"

"No. I heard music but I didn't even see anyone up there."

"Well, that's not surprising. The two men work night shifts. And Mrs. Wantz doesn't move around much since she broke her ankle. She favors it too much, maybe."

"How does she eat?"

"Oh, I cook for her," Louise said. "Of course that costs extra. I'd be willing to do the same for you."

"Well, I get two meals at the motel. That helps out."

As Mari walked to work she thought, *It's getting a little better. I know some people by name now— Liz, Louise, and Ellie, and that Mrs. Wantz I've never even seen yet.*

She met several children as she came to the corner. *There must be an elementary school close to here.* She thought of Wilson School at home. *Are the kids talking about me? Lois Ann will, I know. Should I have told her I was leaving? She'll be real mad at me—if I ever see her or anyone back there again.*

She felt sad all at once, and a little mixed up. *Do I want to be a runaway forever? What's going to happen next and what after that? I never thought about that—just about getting away.*

She went into the lobby by the side door and

smelled food from the direction of the hall which ran past the elevators. *I bet I can get to the kitchen this way. I'll check after I look at the clock.*

A man with black hair mixed with gray was at the desk. He glanced toward Mari and as the telephone rang he said, "I'll be with you later." She sat down in one of the armchairs which were upholstered in green material and looked and felt like leather. The TV behind the desk was on but the sound was so low that she could hear only part of what was being said by the people on the game show. *That's partly because of the cars going by.*

"You want something?" the desk clerk said after he'd finished the telephone conversation.

"No. I'm working here part time. Just wanted to see what time it was. Is it okay if I wait here?"

"No rule against it."

Two girls and a boy walked past the windowed wall of the lobby. They were laughing and Mari suddenly felt a twinge of loneliness. *They're my age—about the first teenagers I've seen here. I guess I'll not get to know many other kids—since I'm not in school.*

Mari picked up her shoulder bag and hurried through the dining room. It was over half full and Liz and another waitress were unloading trays at separate tables. *It won't hurt anything if I begin work a little ahead of time. Being busy is better than sitting around and thinking. Sometimes it is anyway.*

She changed into a uniform. Someone, probably Ellie, had written Mari's name on a piece of paper and pinned it on the collar. *It fits real good. I like the way it looks on me.* She dreaded going out into the kitchen, being the only new person around. *I'll probably make mistakes and break some dishes and everyone will look at me.*

She thought of her mother. *Did she feel like this when she went to work at the motel? She'd been at home for years and years. I never thought of it before that it might have been hard for Mom. She didn't say much about it, and I didn't even think how she might feel.*

She took a deep breath and walked out of the rest room. *I might as well get it over with. No one can do this for me. And I can't quit a job before I start it. That wouldn't be too smart.*

Chapter 4

The next hour and a half seemed to go in a hurry. Mari had no trouble supplying clean dishes and silverware. *It's sort of funny,* she thought as she stacked plates in the wooden tray. *I never thought about it before, but now I know why these trays are made of wood. Because hot water doesn't melt them like it would some plastic, and dishes don't break as easy as they would being banged against metal.*

As she caught up with the waitresses she looked around. *I wonder who is supposed to wash the pans. They're piling up back there in that sink.* Her question was answered when she heard a whistle above the hissing of the steam and the rushing of the motor of the dishwasher. She glanced toward the back of the kitchen and saw someone bending over one end of the double sink. *Whoever it is—she's in a good mood—or he.*

Liz came up to Mari a little before one-thirty. "I'm going off duty now. Will I see you tomorrow?"

"Yes, if you're here at noon. Say, if you're not in too big a hurry—"

"I'm not. What's on your mind?"

Mari told Liz that Ellie hadn't mentioned money—not how much, nor when.

"She will, but I can tell you how it is. At first you get the minimum wage. It's about $2.50 an hour now or maybe a little more. We get paid on Friday. But if you're broke, I can spare a little."

"Oh no. I've still got some, and Friday's only three days away."

"Don't I know! We not only count the days here. We figure up the hours sometimes when we've spent more than we should. Well, I'd better go. It's time to pick up my little one at the day nursery."

As Mari hung the waterproof apron on a hook someone asked, "Are you new too?"

She turned and saw that the pan-washer was a tall boy with copper-red hair. She hadn't caught a good glimpse of him when he was bent over the sink.

"Yes," she said. "It's my first day."

As Mari hung the waterproof apron on a hook someone asked, "Are you new too?" She turned and saw that the pan-washer was a tall boy with copper-red hair.

"It's my second," he told her. "I had to look a long time for this job. Work's hard to find if you never finished high school."

"That's what I hear," Mari said. She walked away, not wanting to hear anymore about school, or be expected to answer any questions. *I really didn't want to quit school,* she thought. *It was good most of the time—especially some classes like Mr. Harrison's. And Mrs. Lederer—even if it wasn't part of her job as counselor, she'd still care what happened to me. She sort of understood when I talked about Dad's drinking. Maybe she saw the bruises on me.*

She met Ellie as she went toward the lobby. "You eating now?"

"No. I thought I'd wait until evening. Should I eat before or after I run the dishwasher?"

"You'd better come in before—say at six or a quarter after. You'll work from seven until eight-thirty. Did I tell you about pay?"

"No. But Liz did. She's real nice."

"That she is," Ellie said. "She's my mainstay. If I ever decide to quit she could take over and no one would be able to tell the difference. They might even see improvement."

Well, what am I going to do with myself until six o'clock? Mari thought as she walked toward her room. *For one thing I'd better get a sandwich to take back. That and an orange will hold me until evening.*

The lower floor seemed empty as she started upstairs. The television screen was dark and there were no sounds or smell of food. *Louise said I could watch TV. But did she mean only with her? Besides, I'd better eat this cheeseburger while it's still a little warm.*

The first door Mari passed was partly open. She wanted to peek in but didn't dare. *That was something Mom couldn't stand—peeking in doors and windows. She said listening on the party-line telephone was just as bad—nosing into other people's business.*

Thoughts of her mother flooded Mari's mind as she ate the sandwich and peeled and sectioned the orange. Was she really worried? *Will Dad blame Mom because I'm gone and make it a lot harder on her? It doesn't seem like he would, because he's the one who didn't want a girl. Mom naming me for him, only changing the "o" in Marion to "a," didn't make me a boy. Maybe they'll get along better if I'm not there. I guess this is the time for them to find out. I'm giving them a chance.*

She had a left-out feeling. *But I had that a lot when I was at home.*

As she gathered up the orange peeling and seeds someone tapped on the door. *Who could be looking for me? Surely not a policeman! No one could find me already, could they?*

She opened the door a few inches and saw a small woman with curly white har. She was leaning on a cane with a silver handle. "Excuse me," she said. "I'm Emilie Wantz."

"Oh, you live across the hall."

"True. And you're—Marianne, is it?"

"Marian. But most people call me Mari. You want to come in?"

31

"Oh, no. I'll tell you why I bothered you. Louise went to her church meeting, a carry-in lunch. She fixed me a tray, but I can see the sign on that hamburger stand and it makes my mouth water."

"I could get one for you," Mari said. "I'd be glad to, and anything else you need."

"Well, that's fine. I'll hobble back to my room for some money. How much will it take?"

"That depends on which sign you're seeing. Crockett's costs more than the McDonalds across the street."

·"No oftener than I allow myself a treat, I'll take the best. And I want you to get one for yourself."

"No, ma'm. Thank you, but I just ate."

"Well, I want you to at least buy a cold drink for yourself for your trouble."

It's no trouble, Mari thought as she left the house. *I'm glad to have something to do. I guess that's kind of a switch for me. I did a lot of grouching sometimes when Mom needed help. But not always, I hope.*

She sipped from the small paper cup on the way back, walking fast so the sandwich wouldn't get cold. *But they wrap them in gold foil, not just thin waxed paper.*

"Won't you come in and keep me company?" Mrs. Wantz said. "Days get long when I can't get out."

"Is your ankle getting any better?"

"Yes. But it's slow. Sit down over here on the couch. You sure you aren't hungry?"

"I'm sure. I still have some Coke." Mari looked around. "Your room's bigger than mine."

"It wasn't when I came here. There was a small

room over on that side there. It was used for storage. After Lou saw I was a permanent boarder we put our heads together, shared the carpenter's fee, and made more room. There's a big closet in the corner."

Mari wanted to ask questions. Didn't Mrs. Wantz have children? Any family? Wouldn't she like to have a place of her own? Was this cheaper? But she decided that asking questions wasn't a good idea right now. Mrs. Wantz might turn around and want to know more about *her*.

"You have a lot of books," Mari said.

"Yes, that's one reason I wanted more room. I'd give up a lot before I'd let go of my books. Do you like to read?"

"Yes," Mari said, "more than most kids I run around with."

"Then help yourself if you see anything that interests you."

"Thank you," Mari said. "I'd like that. And I'll take good care of them."

"If I didn't think you would, I wouldn't have made the offer."

How can she tell I'm trustworthy? Mari wondered. *Is this something people learn, or do they guess?* She chose two books. One was old and looked as if it had been read several times. She asked Mrs. Wantz, "This *Northwest Passage*, is it about history?"

"Yes. It's a story of great courage. Do you like history?"

"Pretty much. It was my favorite subject. This book's thick, but I might like it."

As she started toward the door Mari glanced toward Mrs. Wantz's clock. *Three-thirty already. It won't seem so long before I'm to go back to the motel.*

She decided to take a bath and brush her hair and dress before she began to read. *Tonight I'd better wash my hair. Shampoo! That's something else I'll have to buy. And tomorrow, I'd better find a place to get some hose. These can't hold out much longer.*

She did some multiplying and subtracting as she got ready to go to work. *Three times $2.50, if that's what I get, and three times that for the three days I'll work. That's more than twenty dollars. I'll give Louise another ten. I'll get by for another week. Then I'll have—I don't know how much. Will I work weekends? I'm not used to looking ahead, trying to figure what I can spend and how far money will go.*

Chapter 5

Ellie was the only person Mari knew when she went to work. The tall boy wasn't at the pan sink, Liz was off work, and she hadn't been introduced to the waitresses who came in the afternoon. She ate at a table in the corner, taking care to choose food that was not the most expensive. *I don't remember thinking too much before about the cost of what I ate. Mom talked about it a lot but I guess I didn't pay much attention—not even to Dad yelling at her when she had to ask for money.*

She ate the toasted cheese sandwich first, because the tomato soup needed to cool. *I guess I splurged for sure, getting lemon pie for dessert. But it looks delish!* She watched people at the other tables. *Some are alone—like me. I wonder if that's the way they want things to be?*

Some people in the groups were talking and laughing and seemed to be having a good time. A few just ate with a blank look on their faces, but one woman cried as she buttered a roll. Tears moved down her cheeks and she didn't bother to wipe them away. *What's wrong with her? I doubt that she's worried about money, not with a fur coat and those diamond rings and earrings. Anyway, they look real.*

A woman washed the pans that evening. She didn't say anything to Mari or to anyone except to tell a waitress, "Hear me? Don't dump any more in here."

Mari felt a little afraid as she left the motel. It was dark except for the street lights and the light which came from the sliver of moon. *I might as well get used to it, I guess. Anyway, if someone at the motel offered me a ride they might get curious why I'm in a rooming house. Or do people know that much about places around here? This is a real big city and they could come from other parts of it.*

Louise was watching television and she asked Mari if she wanted to stay downstairs for a while. "Yes, I believe I will. Thank you."

During the first commercial Louise said, "Emilie told me you'd done her a favor. She was real grateful."

"Well, it wasn't much. I was glad to do it. Besides, she loaned me some books."

36

"She surely does treasure her books. I think she'd go hungry before she'd drop her book club subscription."

Mari stayed with Louise for over an hour. In that time she heard that Louise and Emilie had been friends for a long time. "I got married and widowed. Em stayed with her father and took care of him while his savings dribbled away. A lot of his money went for doctor's bills. After he died, she came here until she could get her feet planted solid. And she's stayed. I'd miss her."

Mari began to feel sleepy. "I'd better go," she said. "I should wash my hair." Then she remembered. *I don't have any shampoo. But I'm not going to say that. It would sound like I'm hinting, or begging.*

"Did you look in the medicine cabinet?" Louise asked. "Sometimes folks leave things. There could be something for hair."

Did she know what I was thinking?

"Thank you. I didn't look," Mari said. As she walked to the archway between the living room and the hall she heard the voice from the television saying, "A million beds won't be slept in tonight." *That's about runaways. I've got to get upstairs.* Without turning she said, "Thanks again, Louise. Goodnight."

Tears blinded her as she hurried to her room. *I sure hope I don't run onto anyone and have to answer questions.*

This is the first time I've cried since I skipped out, she thought as she walked to the window. She pushed one panel of lacy curtain back. The streetlight seemed to be moving in water. *That's because of the tears.*

She started toward the bed. *No, I'd better not. I'll cry myself to sleep.* She went to the half bath and found a tube with a fat place at the end. *There's enough shampoo in there for once—maybe twice."*

As she lathered and rinsed she cried and her tears mixed with the water. She rubbed her hair with a towel until no drips fell on her shoulders. She opened the dresser drawer and took out one finger of the Twinkie, tucking the end of the plastic wrapper so the other half wouldn't dry out. She ate and wished she'd bought another can of Coke. *Even warm, it's not so bad.*

As she rolled her hair up on the plastic curlers she thought about the days before she left home. *After Dad whipped me that last time it was like I was kind of numb. I didn't feel anything. I moved as if in a bad dream. If Mom had stood up to him— Oh, well! No use to think about that now. She never did—or almost never.*

Her arms ached by the time she'd finished. She rested them on the chair arms and brought her hands up to her shoulders several times. *If Mom had been home when the attendance clerk checked on me, would I be here now? Or would Dad have found something else to belt me about? It never took much when he was drunk.* She remembered the time she'd tried to talk to her mother about the whiskey. "Doesn't it cost a lot?"

"Yes, I guess," her mother said, "and there's plenty of things we need worse."

"Why don't you say so then?" Mari asked.

Mom didn't answer. Just shook her head and went to the kitchen or somewhere. It wasn't long after that she began to do ironings.

For the first time Mari wondered why her mother had asked for a job at the motel. *She was always kind of—well, shy—about getting out where people were. She always said she wasn't a good mixer. Then why did she decide to go to work? Did something happen that I don't know about? Something to make her stand up for herself? But not for me?*

She looked at her checked dress as she hung it in the closet. *I'm giving this real hard wear. Is there a laundromat here someplace? Maybe I'd better ask if I can wear jeans to work. It'd take me a while to save up money for another dress. That pink one's too fancy. Where would I ever wear it here?*

She was in bed before she thought again of the television announcement about runaways. *I wonder what else it said? Why was it on the air? I'd like for Mom to know I'm not hurt or anything. Not in any kind of trouble—so far. But where'd I be if I didn't have any money? To pay for a room or something to eat?*

She was wakened by the sound of a siren. At first she thought it was part of a dream she was having. It was like she was walking, sort of uphill toward a house, a white house with shining windows and flower boxes in every one. All the flowers were either pink or white. As Mari walked the house moved back, and the faster she moved the farther away it was. She was getting very tired when she opened her eyes and knew that the house she never reached was in a dream and that the wail of the siren was real. She went to the window and couldn't see anything. She heard uneven footsteps in the hall and tiptoed to the door. She opened it a little and saw Mrs. Wantz moving toward the head of the stairs.

"What's going on?" Mari asked as she caught up with her.

"Oh, it's a fire. I could see the red sky from my window."

"I hope it's not the motel," Mari said.

"Oh no. It's farther away. But I just couldn't go back to sleep. I thought maybe Lou wouldn't care if I made a cup of hot chocolate. Warm milk's supposed to help you sleep, but the thought of it without some flavoring gags me."

"If you think Louise won't care, I could make it and bring it up," Mari offered.

"Well—no. I'm going down. I've let myself be shut up too long. I've made my own prison. But I'd appreciate it if you'd go down with me and give me a steadying hand."

"I'll wait here," Mari said when they reached the living room.

"Sure you won't have a cup with me?"

"No. I'm not one bit hungry."

"Then turn on the TV," Mrs. Wantz said. "Lou sleeps in the back of the house. It won't wake her."

Is anything on? Mari thought. *What time is it?* She dialed the late talk show and turned to another station. *No use to get interested in what they're saying. I'm not going to be down here that long.* She stopped when she heard the word runaways. "Let someone know you're all right." Then a number flashed on the screen. *Toll-free, it says. Who would I get? How does that work? I haven't heard enough about it to be sure.*

Chapter 6

The sun was above the tops of the houses across the street when Mari opened her eyes the next morning. *I must have really slept in,* she thought as she reached for the radio. *If these batteries play out I'll never know the time of day. Seems like a lot of ways to spend money keep coming up.* She doubled the pillow and looked toward the window as she listened to two songs—until she heard, "Stay tuned for the nine o'clock news."

I'd better get going. I'll get myself something to eat, maybe, at that drugstore. And I'll find a place to buy hose and spare batteries. And it wouldn't hurt to get some more snacks. There's only one orange left and half a Twinkie.

She decided to put on her clean pair of jeans. *I can go past and ask Ellie if it's okay to wear them. It seems like it would be, since I change into a uniform.*

Louise was sweeping the front steps. When Mari saw her she almost asked, "Is there a shopping center somewhere close?" Then she thought, *If I put it that way she may get curious about why I don't already know. She might ask where I came from and what I'm doing here.* So she said, "Where do you buy hose, Louise? Is one place better than the other or are they about all the same?"

Louise let the broom fall. The handle bounced with a clattering sound when it hit the steps. As she reached up to take out two hairpins and refasten the back of her up-sweep hairdo, Louise said, "I can tell you where I go for me and Emilie. To Southgate Mall—the department store. The 99-centers wear me as well or even a little better than some that come in fancier packages."

How can I get to Southgate Mall? Mari was wondering when Louise said, "If you hurry you'll catch the bus that stops catercornered from the motel. Say, would you mind getting me some hairpins like this one? I shed them like this old broom is losing its straws. Have I got any change in these pockets?"

"You can pay me later," Mari said. "Thanks, Louise."

Three people were waiting at the corner under the bus stop sign. *I don't see any coming,* Mari thought. *How will I know which one to take?* She wished she had time to run across and ask Ellie or someone if there was any rule about what to wear to work. *I don't want to get myself in trouble by doing something wrong.* Then a feeling of sadness made her turn back and walk a few steps away from the three people. *Who am I kidding? Being here is breaking rules. Skipping school, taking money from Mom, running away, letting people think I'm older—if they do. But I can't think about all that now.*

One of her questions was answered when a yellow and orange bus pulled to the curb with the brakes hissing. The sign on the front said "Southgate Mall." As she handed coins to the driver she asked, "Which bus will I take to get back here?"

"Keystone Avenue," he said without looking up.

Is that the name of this street or the one Louise lives on? I didn't pay any attention.

As she looked out the window she hoped the mall wasn't clear across the city. *I don't have all day. But Louise knows I'm to be at work at twelve. She wouldn't have pointed me to somewhere too far away.* An uneasy feeling in her stomach made her realize that she hadn't had breakfast. *There wasn't time. I'll have to see if there's a place out here. I'll be starved before I get back to work. Seems like something to worry about keeps coming up. I never noticed that before. Not so much.*

The shopping center was about the same size as the plaza near Mari's home. *They probably have bigger ones here somewhere.* She saw the department store entrance as soon as she walked through the swinging doors. She'd slipped two dollars into one pocket of her jeans. *No use letting anyone know I have money down in the bottom of this bag.* She'd heard a lot of rip-off stories. *Kids who have a lot better clothes than me, who didn't really need to steal, take things. Probably for kicks, or to buy drugs.*

She glanced at the clock at the back of the store before going to find a place to eat. She had over half an hour. She found a lunch counter in what the kids at home called a five to fifty store. *Only I don't know why. What costs only five cents?*

She ordered orange juice and cooked oatmeal and toast. *That'll take what's left of the two dollars.* The hot cereal didn't taste as good to Mari as what she had at home. *We cooked ours. They just poured hot water on this. But it's food.*

She passed a group of people as she hurried toward the exit. She glanced at them just long enough to see that some were boys. One had long hair, bound to his head with a bright green band. Two girls were barefoot, and one was wearing denim overalls without any blouse at all. *That's really trashy.*

As Mari turned toward the four glass doors someone said, "Hey! Don't I know you?"

Mari felt her throat tighten as she spun around and said, "Well, I don't know you." Yet there was *something* familiar.

"Sure! I saw you back in Castleton last week at that hangout for straights. The Candy Box."

Mari wanted to run. *And it's not just because this girl's been at home. It's something else.*

45

"You left while I was pouring it on those dumb kids. Man it was worth being stuck there to see the looks on their faces."

I know now, Mari thought. *She was telling the tricks of getting along when you're on your own.*

"You live here or there? By the way, I'm Buffy." Before Mari could decide on an answer the girl asked, "Or in between?"

"I'm staying here now."

"Any problems? Like money? Or finding a pad?"

"No. I'm fine."

"Want to come back and meet The Group?"

"I'd better not," Mari said. "I have a bus to catch."

"Suit yourself. But if things go sour, come around. Some of us make this our meeting place, when we don't need a real hideout.

"Thanks," Mari said.

As she rode toward the motel Mari tried to remember exactly what she'd said. *I didn't tell her my name and as far as I know she's never heard it. I said I'm staying here. But I've got a feeling that Buffy knows I'm a runaway. I don't think I want to get mixed up with her. She doesn't look as bad as some of the others, except her eyes are sort of hard.*

A lot of questions came to her as she leaned her cheek against the quivering glass of the bus window. Did runaways have ways of knowing each other? How did the idea of making the mall a meeting place come about? Are they the same kind of

Mari felt her throat tighten as she spun around and said, "Well, I don't know you." Yet there was something familiar about her.

kids or do they stick together because they're runaways? She felt a little mixed up. It would be nice to meet some kids and have friends her own age. *Ellie and Liz and Emilie and Louise are real nice to me. But I'm kind of lonesome. Maybe I'll go back over there and see if there's anyone I'd like. Just maybe.*

She walked into the motel at fifteen till twelve and looked for Liz as she went through the dining room. She met her at the door which opened into the kitchen. "I began to worry if you were going to have time to eat," Liz said.

"I'll wait until afterward. I had my breakfast only a little while ago. I was wondering. Will Ellie care if I wear these to work?"

Liz looked Mari over, turned her around, and said, "You're fine. But if those jeans were ragged and your hair stringy it would be a different story. I've seen people not hired or fired, for such things."

Mari headed into the kitchen. "I see you made it," the pan boy said.

"I meant to," Mari said. "You only work noons?"

"Yep. Except on Saturday. Do you work then?"

"I don't know. Ellie didn't say."

"I play baseball at school. I work here instead of going home noon hours. Same with you?"

"In a way," Mari said.

She didn't hurry with her lunch. There wasn't any reason to get back to the room. She listened to the other two waitresses who took their noon break at the same time, as she ate chicken and dumplings and cottage cheese with peaches. They talked about how much they'd received in tips and what

48

they had to do at home. The tall one whose name was Ardith asked, "Was the fur-and-diamond gal in any better spirits today?"

"No. She can't seem to stop crying. Not for long, anyway."

"I saw her yesterday," Mari said. "Does anyone know what's wrong with her?"

"Oh, yes," Ardith said. "They were guests here. Her husband's a salesman. He had a heart attack in their room about a week ago. A bad one. He's in intensive care at the hospital. She can't see him except for a few minutes every few hours."

As Mari carried her tray to the kitchen she thought, *That's really bad, being way off from wherever home is and getting sick.* She felt shivery, an all-at-once coldness. As she walked to the motel lobby she let herself think of what she'd do if she was back in Castleton. Before that she'd not wanted to think much about home. *For one thing I'd be in school. And any dishwashing I'd do would be for Mom. Seems I think of her a lot. I wonder if Buffy and her friends think about their folks.*

She went out to the lobby and watched most of a game show on TV before leaving the motel. Taxis pulled up to let some people out and others took people away. A bus stopped at the main doors and at least twenty women stepped out and began coming into the lobby. *No use trying to watch a program now, not with all that talking. I wonder where they're from and why they're here.* For the first time Mari wondered if people from Castleton ever stayed at the motel. Would they if home was only eighty miles away?

Chapter 7

Mari wished she could think of something to do between her noon and evening work shifts. *I have the books Mrs. Wantz loaned me. But I'll have all evening to read. I know for sure I don't want to go prowling around at night, and get picked up—not by anyone.*

She went to the lobby and sat on the couch. Someone had left a newspaper on one end. *It's not the* Courier, *so I probably won't know anyone it mentions.* She read the comic strips, which weren't funny, and looked at the picture of the girls who were getting married. *I wonder if that's what they want for sure? Or are they just trying to get away, like Patty? I haven't heard anything about her for a long time. Mom says Aunt Edna never speaks her name. Does Mom mention mine? I bet Dad does— but loud!*

Ellie came through the lobby and stopped at the outside door. "Are you busy for an hour or so? Do you have anything to do?"

"No, nothing much."

"Well, I'm going out in the country to get eggs from a farm. I'd be glad to have some company."

Mari wanted to go and it was only after she said yes and followed Ellie to the parking lot that she felt a little uneasy. Would it be harder to get out of answering questions if she was shut up in a car?

After they reached the farm and Ellie hadn't pried, Mari relaxed and enjoyed herself. She walked along a white board fence while Ellie went inside the green-shingled house. She stopped and looked at the furry buds of a pussy willow tree. *Spring's really on its way when these show up. I used to see them on the way to school, in Mr. Prentiss' yard.*

She glanced across the road and saw a girl walking toward a mailbox. Instead of stopping to look in the metal box she kept on coming. *That's Patty! She's seen me. And I can't get away.*

"Marian! What are you doing here?"

After glancing back at the house Mari hurried to the fence along the road. "Please, Pat. Don't give me away."

"Well, I wasn't thinking about doing that. You've run away from home?"

"Yes."

"Does anyone back in Castleton know where you are?"

"No. I just couldn't take another beating."

"I remember how Uncle Bud acted. I was always scared of him. But first, do you have a place to stay?"

The words tumbled out. The girls tried to get as much said as possible after Mari said she'd have to leave any minute. When Ellie climbed into the car Patty said, "I do have a telephone. I'm in the book. Look for Jay Conley—he's my husband. Oh, I wish I could have you here."

"You won't tell anyone at home?"

"Marian, I don't talk to anyone in Castleton—not one person. Call me."

"You see someone you know?" Ellie asked as they left the farm.

"Yes, Patty Conley. She used to live close to me." She didn't think it would be wise to say that Patty was her cousin and that the place they'd lived was Castleton.

"Here," Ellie said as she picked up a small paper bag from the seat. "Mrs. Dane was making cookies—old-fashioned molasses. Take a couple."

"They're still warm."

"I know. She insisted that I wait until the first tray came out of the oven. Want me to drop you off somewhere?"

"What time is it?"

"Nearly three."

"Then I'll get out at the motel. I have a few errands to run in that neighborhood."

As Mari held the door open for Ellie and the half case of eggs, she said, "Thanks for asking me to go along." She walked slowly toward the Jiffy Market, thinking about Patty all the time. *She looks older. She was always thin, but now she's really skinny. And sort of unhappy. I guess getting married didn't solve all her problems. Anyway, I'm glad I can call her. Should I use Louise's phone or go to a booth?*

Maybe I'd better count my money, Mari thought as she paid for three apples (two red and one yellow), a small package of cheese, a half-pound box of soda crackers, and two cans of pop. *Tomorrow's payday, but I still have to be careful.*

She ate the other half of the Twinkie as she sat on the edge of the tub and waited for it to fill. *At home Dad would be yelling, asking who I thought was going to pay for the water I used. One of his stupid questions.*

Before going back to her room Mari went to the head of the stairs and listened.

"That you, Mari?" Mrs. Wantz said from her room.

"Yes'm. I was wondering. Is Louise here?"

"No, she went grocery shopping. Do you need something?" Mrs. Wantz asked.

"Not really. But if *you* want to use the telephone, what do you do?"

"Oh, I have an extension. Didn't Louise tell you about the pay phone in the coat closet?"

"The coat closet?"

"Yes, in the front hall on the back wall. Of course no one puts coats in there these days. Lou had the carpenter put a little bench on the side when he was making my room larger. There's a light. You have to pull the string."

"Thank you," Mari said. "Do you need anything today?"

"No, I'm pretty well fixed. Lou took my wish list like she does every Thursday. And believe it or not I'm eating out tonight."

"That's great."

"Yes, the church circle is having a little banquet over across town somewhere. I'm going to get dressed up, hobble downstairs, and ride along."

"Well, have a good time," Mari said. "I'll get some change and make my phone call."

I don't know why I'm in such a hurry to talk to Patty. She's older and we weren't ever real close. Her family and mine didn't visit much, not after Dad told Aunt Edna she must have been vaccinated with a phonograph needle. I don't think she and Mom got together much after that, except on the telephone when Dad was away.

When Patty said hello, Mari asked, "Is this a bad time to call?"

"No, this is the best time. Jay works at the factory from two to eleven. I hoped I'd hear from you. I really have been thinking about you. I've got all sorts of questions. If you don't want to answer, just say so."

"I don't mind. But I have to be careful here, or people will catch on I'm a runaway and report me to someone." She told her cousin about her room and her job, even that she'd taken a twenty-dollar bill from her mother's hiding place, taped under one of the shelves of the pan cupboard. "I sure hated doing that. It wouldn't have bothered me to take it from Dad, but there was no way to do that."

"We both know it's wrong to steal," Patty reminded her, "but it's good you could rent a room."

"I know. It scares me when I think where I'd be, or what I'd be doing for money if I couldn't have paid to stay in this place."

"Maybe if Aunt Bertie knew how some runaways have to live she'd be glad you had some money."

"I never thought of that," Mari said. "Say, did I hear a baby?"

"Yes. You didn't know? That's Heidi. She's over a year old already. I named her for a girl in a book."

"I've read *Heidi*. I liked it too. Do you need to check on her now?"

"Not yet. She's playing in her pen." Then Patty began to cry. Mari could hear the choking sobs. She waited until her cousin could talk. "Oh, Marian, that's what I'm in, a pen, a kind of prison. I never said that to anyone before. But Jay—well, he didn't really want to marry me. I'd know it even if he didn't keep saying it. And I can't go home and how can I support myself and take care of my baby? Maybe there's a way. But I can't see it."

"I didn't mean to make you feel bad," Mari said.

"It wasn't you. And already I feel a little better. You don't know how it is not having anyone I can talk to—anyone I know."

"I'm beginning to find that out too. People here are real good to me, here in the rooming house and at work. But there's a lot I can't say."

"Are there any kids your age?"

"Just a boy. He washes pans at noon for an hour.

I saw some kids over at the shopping center, but I don't know if I want to hook up with them."

"I wish I could have you out here. But Jay seems to enjoy saying mean things to me when people are here. More than usual."

"That's the way my dad is."

"But sometimes I get the pickup truck when Jay sleeps late. And a lot of times he goes fishing. Do you suppose it would hurt anything if I stopped by?"

"I don't see how it could. I can say you're my cousin—which is the truth. And I'd get to see Heidi that way. Tomorrow'd be fine. I get paid. We could go to Crockett's maybe."

"Let's leave it this way. You call me about one. And I'll know by then if Jay's going to be away. It's payday for him too."

"Make it one-thirty. I get off work then. See you tomorrow, I hope."

Mari had talked so long that she had to hurry to get to the motel in time to eat her evening meal before going to work. *But that's okay. This has been a better day than any I've had for a long time.*

As she worked she thought about how it had been at home. *Everything wasn't bad. I could go to Lois Ann's or the Candy Box if I had a little money. That helped, like talking to Patty. It gets your mind on something else—like I'd better get my mind on my business right now.*

Chapter 8

Mari read until she was sleepy that night. She wound up the bluebird music box several times between chapters. The book about some men on an expedition to find a northwest passage made her feel glad to be in a clean warm bed, even if it wasn't in a real home. Sometimes the explorers were so tired they had to sleep in trees above the watery swamps.

She heard the sound of a vacuum cleaner at the end of the hall when she opened her eyes the next morning. *This must be the day Louise cleans.* She looked around and thought, *I've not been too messy.*

Then she pulled on a pair of jeans and slipped a tee shirt over her head before going to the door. She waited until Louise turned and saw her. *No need to walk out and scare her.*

"Good morning. Did I wake you?"

"I'm not sure. Anyhow, it's time. I was thinking, I could do my room if it's okay."

"Well, sure thing. But you pay for it. Is there any way I could even things up?"

"That doesn't matter— but if you want to keep it straight, I need a few things washed. There's not much."

"Then gather it up while I finish cleaning Mr. Springer's room. That man! No matter how many ashtrays I put in here he fills them up. Thank goodness he uses them."

"Do you need this sweeper downstairs before I use it?" Mari asked as they met in the hall.

"No. I keep this one in that old wardrobe down the hall. This and furniture polish and dust cloths and such. That big chest was my mother's. I remember the day it was moved up here. I thought the van men were going to have to tear down the stair railing. I don't set any store by it now, but I wouldn't have the heart to ask anyone to get it out. Here, let me take your dirty clothes. Is this all of it?"

"Yes, except for a dress. And it probably ought to be done by itself."

"Well go ahead and get it. And yank the sheets and pillowcases off your bed while you're at it. I might as well do things up right. There's clean ones on the upper shelf of the wardrobe."

Mari took time to eat an apple and a few crackers with a chunk of cheese before cleaning the room. She opened the window a few inches and a soft breeze made the curtains dance. *It'll look nice in here if Patty gets to town and has time to come up.*

Ellie was at the cash register when Mari walked through the dining room. She crooked a finger when she saw Mari. "Any objections to getting paid?"

"Can't think of a single one," Mari said.

"Here you are. It's not a full week's pay, of course. Can you make it?"

"Yes. Thank you."

"No need to say thanks. You've earned it. Oh, I almost forgot. Do you want to work Saturday or Sunday?"

"You mean either or both?"

"Which one? I wouldn't expect you to break into both days."

Mari wanted to say, "Break into what?" but she didn't want to give away the fact that she was on her own. "I guess Saturday would be best for me."

"Fine," Ellie said. "Now sometimes we're real busy Saturday evenings, and you might not get off quite as early."

"That's okay. I'll be here tomorrow."

Mari took time to count her money before she changed into her uniform. *"It's a little more than I thought. I can pay Louise and get by. But no big spending.*

When the last stack of clean plates was on the dish counter Mari hurried to the pay phone in the lobby. "You must have been right there," she said when Patty answered the two rings.

"I was. And I can come. Jay's gone for I don't know how long. Overnight anyway. And the truck's here."

"You want to come to my room? It's not too hard to find. 4117 South Keystone. Is that far for you?"

"Not too far. At least it's on the same side of the city. I can be there in an hour or less."

Mari had decided to wear her pink dress but when she got back to her room she saw that Louise had hung the black and white dress on a hook outside her door. The rest of her clothes were folded and stacked in a cardboard box. *This will be better*, she thought as she slipped the white-collared dress over her head. *I wonder if I'll ever wear that pink one anyplace here?*

She went downstairs to wait for Patty. Louise wasn't in sight as Mari went out and sat on the top step. *I wonder which way Patty will come? All I know is to watch for a pickup truck. I don't even know what color it is.*

She heard her cousin before she saw her. With four beeps of the horn, Patty pulled the bright yellow truck to the curb across the street. Mari walked over to welcome her. "Want to come up and see my room now or wait till later?"

"Now would be better," Patty said. She stepped down and turned to lift her little girl from a car seat.

"It seems kind of funny to see you with a baby," Mari said.

"You mean funny peculiar or funny ha ha? Remember that cartoon?"

"I remember," Mari said. "She's cute. Could I carry her? Would she let me?"

"I think so. She's a happy baby—which helps me."

"Is anyone at home here?" Patty asked as they walked upstairs. "Anyone that Heidi would bother?"

"Just Mrs. Wantz in that room. I hear her TV. The two men work. I never have seen or heard them—just their footsteps."

The girls sat on the edge of the bed watching Heidi as she crawled around. "I see they have a music box like yours," Patty said.

"It *is* mine. I brought it with me."

Patty took a long breath. "You know what I was thinking on the way in? I wish we could shove the bad things out of our minds and just have a good time for awhile."

"Okay by me," Mari said. "Do you have to be back any certain time?"

"Well, I'd better get there before dark. For one thing that truck sort of sputters and I wouldn't want to be stuck on the road after dark—not with Heidi. And another thing—Jay's folks live just a little way from us. They keep an eye on me—not in a good way, either. But I do need to go to the shopping center. I've done some babysitting and would like to get Heidi a dress and me a pair of sneakers."

"There's a mall not far from here. I went on the bus."

"I know. I've been there."

The girls didn't talk on the way to the mall. The truck motor was noisy and Patty seemed on edge about driving. "This big place scares me," she said. "It's not like Castleton where I knew every street."

"You have to get anything here?" Patty asked as they crossed the parking lot.

"Just batteries for my radio. That's how I tell time. Shall I carry Heidi so you can look around?"

"You could, but let's look for a place where they have small shopping carts. I brought this blanket for padding. Wire seats can't be too comfortable." They walked through one department store, shifting Heidi from one pair of arms to the other. "There's a drugstore on that side," Patty said. "They have carts."

"Why don't I take her, get my batteries, then ride her up and down out here as long as she's happy?"

"Are you sure you don't mind?"

"Of course I'm sure. Take your time."

Mari pushed the cart the full length of the concourse on one side of the brick walls with planters for artificial vines and with stone benches. She had started up the other side before she thought of Buffy and her groupies. She was turning the cart around when she saw the girl she'd first heard in the Candy box in Castleton coming toward her.

"Taken to kidnapping?" she said.

"Just walking her for someone."

"Well, that's one way to get bread. You doing okay?"

"Yes. I'm okay."

"I can't say the same. Oh, we've got a pad. Herbie—he's over there—has a room all of us share. But no one's got a job now. And the chances of a rip-off are few and far between. They've spread the word about us. Happen to have a cigarette?"

"Yes, I do," Mari said. She felt around in her denim bag without taking it from her shoulder. "Here, take these."

"These all you got? You don't want to keep any?"

"No. I don't really smoke. I've never got to liking it. I just grabbed those up when I left home."

"I suppose you don't have any spare cash?"

"No, not really. I'd better be going."

As she went to meet Patty she thought, *I know one thing for sure. I'm not coming out here alone. Never. I don't want to get mixed up with Buffy and her gang. I don't like the way she makes me feel. Besides, I have Patty to talk to now. Buffy scares me. If being runaway means living like she does— well, I'll think about that later. Like Patty says, we're going to shove bad things out of our minds today.*

Patty looked a little happier when she came out of the department store. "Was I lucky! They were having a sale. I have nearly four dollars left. Such a fortune! But it is a lot to me. I can buy a couple of magazines and a ball for Heidi. My father-in-law's beagle chewed her other one. And I'll still have eating money."

"I meant to treat you," Mari said, "for hauling me around."

"Don't you know that *you* are a treat to me?" Patty said. "Knowing you live close by and getting to run around a little. It's almost like—"

"I know what you were going to say," Mari said. "It's almost like being at home."

"Yes, like the good part of life at home."

After the girls ate, feeding Heidi crumbs of buns and bites of strained apricots from a jar, Patty took Mari back to her room. Louise was raking dead grass and twigs from a flower bed. "I want you to meet her. Do you have time?"

"I sure do," Patty said.

"This is my cousin Patty and her little girl," Mari called. "She lives out in the country."

"Well, now, isn't it nice you girls could get together," Louise said as she walked to the grass between the sidewalk and the curb.

"We think so," Patty said.

"I worry about Mari being by herself so much," Louise said. "You come back, or feel free to call."

As Louise returned to the flower bed Patty asked, "Why does she call you Mari?"

"That's what I tell people—Mari with an "i". I guess I don't like to be reminded of my dad when anyone calls my name."

"I understand. I wish you could come home with me while Jay's away."

"I would if I didn't have to work. But I don't want to get fired."

"I wouldn't want that either. Promise me something, Mari. Don't ever move away from here without letting me know. Okay?"

"Okay. 'Bye Heidi. You're *so* cute."

Chapter 9

*T**his has been a pretty good day,*** Mari thought as she left the motel the next evening. *Partly because yesterday was the best—for a long time.* She decided she'd call Patty. *If Jay's there and she can't talk I'll understand and try later.*

Louise was watching television. "Want to join me after you return your call?"

"Call?"

"Your cousin. She said it wasn't urgent—that anytime would do."

"I'll call her right away. She might be lonesome."

"No need to use the pay phone. It's not a toll call.

65

Use mine. It's in the kitchen."

"Are you still by yourself?" Mari asked when she heard Patty's voice.

"Yes, except for Heidi. And the lady across the road came over awhile. She's real nice."

"You mean where Ellie buys eggs?"

"Yes. She brought me some cookies and loaned me a stack of magazines. I feel rich, in a way, with so much to read. What you going to do tomorrow?"

"I don't know. I don't have to work. The day will probably seem long."

"If Jay doesn't come back, I'll come get you. I tell you what. If he's not here, I'll call you by nine and—Oh, Mari! It's no go! He's getting out of his brother's car now."

"Well, call me when you can."

"I certainly will," Patty said. "And you do the same."

"I have the money for the room," Mari told Louise as she went back to the living room and sat down on the flowered sofa.

"It's not due until Tuesday."

"I know, but I might as well pay now."

"Make yourself comfortable and watch the rest of this three-hour special with me," Louise invited. "I think Emilie's going to come down and join us as soon as she takes her bath."

Nearly two hours later Mari leaned over and felt around for her shoes. "I'm getting sleepy and I don't think you two would like the idea of leading me up to bed."

"I'd probably cover you with the afghan and let you sleep on the sofa," Louise said. "I was just thinking a cup of hot chocolate might taste good. Think you can prop your eyelids open that long, Mari?"

"I could try."

"I think I'll go to the kitchen with you," Emilie said. "I've not seen your new curtains. Besides, this ankle of mine needs to be limbered up."

"All of me needs limbering," Louise said, "after I sit in one place that long."

As Mari turned back to look at the television she saw the beginning of the announcement about runaways again, with a girl running down the railroad track. *It never shows her getting anywhere. She just keeps running.* As she listened, Mari found a piece of paper and a ballpoint pen, and when the toll-free number was flashed on the screen she copied it down. *I don't know why. But I guess it won't hurt to have it in case I take a notion to call—*

I'm not sleepy now, Mari thought as she turned down the blanket on the bed she slept in. *I woke myself coming to bed. I wish this room looked more like a living room—like Lois Ann's. How did she do that? I remember! She made the beds join at the corner, one going one way, one the other—more like a couch. I'm going to ask Louise if she'd care. That would give me something to do tomorrow.* As she brushed her hair she had to smile. *Some way to spend a Sunday—moving furniture!*

She couldn't go to sleep. Lots of pictures flashed through her mind. She thought of what she might be doing if she were back in Castleton. *I might call Lois Ann and if she didn't have to go see her aunts with her mother, I'd run over. I might even go along. I did lots of times. If we stayed in town we could listen to records or head for the Candy Box or take a bus and walk through Christy Woods over by the university. I'd like that best.*

Thoughts of home were clear, more so than they'd been any time since she left. Was that because she'd been with Patty? Her feelings about her cousin had changed. *But I'm still sort of mixed up. I know she wishes she hadn't got married. Anybody could tell that. But she sure does love that little Heidi. Will Patty ever go back home? Not in the same way, I guess. Things are so different for her now.*

The words of the announcement about runaways came to her mind, "A million beds won't be slept in tonight." She could picture her room. *Mom really tried to make it nice. She helped me enamel my old furniture and bought gold decals to go with the ivory. She even made the pink ruffled curtains. Does she ever go in there now?*

Mari began to cry. *I guess I'm homesick. Is it possible to miss a place you thought you couldn't stand one more day?* She slipped out of bed, opened the door, and listened. *No one's up. I'm going to do it. What can it hurt if they don't ask any questions like it said on TV?*

She put her denim jacket over her short gown. *I*

She had to talk with a lump in her throat and wondered if the lady could tell she was about to cry. "Tell Mom I'm not doing anything bad, and that I'm not hungry, and I have a nice room."

*might meet someone on the way to the hall closet—
one of those men.* She fished some coins out of the
bottom of her purse. *I'll have to work at least a half
an hour to pay for the calls I've made. Even if the
number is toll-free, I have to get a dial tone.*

She wanted to run downstairs after she found the
number in her denim bag. *No, I'd better not change
my mind. Even if Mom didn't stand up for me I
ought not let her worry—if there's a way to let her
know I'm okay.*

She dialed the number and felt her heart thump-
ing. *Why'm I so scared? All I'm going to do is what
that person said.*

"Peace of Mind," a voice said after Mari heard
several clicking sounds.

What does that mean? Mari thought.

"Is this the right place—to let someone know
you're okay?"

"Yes it is. Whom do you want us to call?"

"My mother, please. Her number is 329-7190, and
the area code's 320."

The person taking the call repeated the number.

"That's right," Mari said. "And please, if a man
answers will you not say anything. Mom works.
And he might not tell her."

"Certainly. We'll do as you ask. Is there anything
else you want your mother to know?"

"Well, yes," Mari said. She had to talk with a
lump in her throat and wondered if the lady could
tell she was about to cry. "Tell Mom I'm not doing
anything bad, and that I'm not hungry, and I have a
nice room."

"That's fine. You must have a job."

"Yes'm, part time. Well, I'd better go. Thanks."

"You call whenever you want to send a message to your mother. But I'll need your name."

Oh, no! Is there a catch to this after all? Are they going to trace me? Mari wondered.

"Just your first name, dear. So your mother will know the message is from you."

"Tell her it's Marian and that almost everyone calls me Mari."

I feel better, letting Mom know, she thought as she went upstairs. *Then why am I crying?*

After a few minutes she heard three knocks on her door. Who could it be? One of the men she hadn't seen?"

"It's Emilie Wantz, Mari. Are you all right?"

"Yes," Mari said. She went to the door but didn't turn on the light. *No need to worry her about my crying.*

"I heard you go downstairs and thought you might have some kind of problem."

"No, I just wanted to let someone know something. I didn't mean to wake anyone."

"Oh, you didn't. My book club selection came today. And Mr. Scott and Mr. Springer aren't here. They never are on weekends. They have a cabin on the lake. You go on back to bed."

Well, I know their names now, Mari thought. *Not that it makes much difference. It just seems funny to live in the same house with people and not know their names. Funny peculiar, like Patty said.* Questions kept her awake. *If Patty had a chance, would she leave Jay? What would she do with Heidi? If a person runs away once, is it easier to do it again?*

71

As she doubled her pillow and turned over on her left side, she thought that leaving home was a lot different than she'd imagined. *It's not one bit exciting. Not for me. I was scared when I hid my suitcase behind the glider on the porch. I was afraid someone would steal it or Dad would come home loaded again and find out I was splitting. It wasn't fun needing to sneak around in the bus station— not wanting to see anyone I know.*

There've been a lot of bad feelings since—like meeting Buffy. And wondering if people at the motel or here would find out I was a runaway and call the police. But the good part is knowing that Liz or Ellie or Louise or Emilie wouldn't do that to me. Or would they? No, I think they'd talk to me first.

I guess running away's not the same for everyone. Not the same for me as it is for Buffy and her group. What would I do if I had to live like she does? Go home? That would be awful hard, because Dad would really lay it on me. But I don't want to think about that.

She raised up and wound the spring on her music box. She couldn't see the china bird perched on a spray of roses and couldn't really see his outspread wings. *But I know how it looks and can hear the music.*

"Sunrise . . . sunset. Sunrise . . . sunset."

Chapter 10

What am I going to do about eating today? Mari thought when she was wide-awake the next morning. *I don't get two free meals on my day off. A whole day's food will take a big bite out of my pay. I can make out for breakfast. I guess no one passed a law saying a person can't eat an apple, cheese, and crackers first thing in the morning.*

She ate, then read until she could hear sounds from downstairs. When Louise turned on a faucet anywhere, gurgling sounds echoed in the pipes in the half bath. Emilie's door was open but she wasn't in sight, until Mari came to the living room.

Mrs. Wantz was wearing a lavender dress and a small hat that looked like a small round box which had been covered with pale pink flowers.

"You look pretty," Mari said. "Must be going someplace."

"I am indeed. Louise invited me to her church. I've missed so much I'm out of the habit. It's hard to get back."

"Is Louise dressing?"

"No. She'll be out any minute. She's checking the timer on the oven. She doesn't quite trust it to work without some prodding from her."

"Good morning, Mari," Louise said as she came from the kitchen. "If I'd known you were up I'd have invited you to go with us. I would now if there were more time."

"That's all right," Mari said. "What I wanted won't keep you but a minute. Is there some rule against rearranging the furniture in my room?"

"Goodness, no," Louise said. "If you wait until we get back, we'll give you a hand."

"Oh, I think I can manage. You two be good now!"

Mari liked the new arrangement. *When beds don't have headboards you can do things like this. The room looks better already. It'd be nice if I had some pretty pillows, though.* As she worked she thought a little about the idea of going to church with Louise. *Will I if they ask me again? I used to like it, but I didn't go much after Mom quit. She never did say why—not that I remember. It was so long ago.*

She hurried to take a bath while she was alone in the house. *I think I'll get a box of fried chicken at*

*that place up the street from the motel and bring it
back here to eat.* She looked for someone she knew
as she passed the drive into which she usually
turned. All she saw were strangers going into the
dining room. *Anyone I know is already on the job.
Maybe I'll come over here and eat tonight even if I
do have to pay. I could even dress up and wear that
pink dress.*

"Did you get your room changed?" Louise called
from the kitchen, when Mari returned to the rooming house.

"Yes. Come see it when you have time."

"I'll be there in a jiffy. I'm taking Emilie's tray
up. She gave her ankle a workout this morning and
doesn't want to come down,"

Will Louise like it that I'm eating up here? Mari
wondered. *It seems sort of strange, three people
eating in three rooms. But it was like that at home
sometimes. When Dad was yelling Mom said she
couldn't swallow. And other days he passed out
from drinking too much and couldn't eat with us.*

She left the door half open and when Louise came
from Emilie's room Mari said, "I'm eating in. Is it
okay?"

"As long as you are careful. Especially since
you're your own cleaning lady. Say, that looks real
cozy."

"Cozy," Mari said. "I've not heard that word for a
long time. One of my girl friends—her grandma
said it a lot."

"It means homelike," Louise said. "At least to me
it does. Know what you need yet? Pillows."

"Sometimes I think you're a mind reader," Mari

said. "Or is it that we think the same?"

"Probably. I've got a big plastic bag of foam pillows downstairs, covered with corduroy. I had a roomer once, a salesman, whose company went broke. When he couldn't pay his rent he gave me his samples. I didn't have the heart to tell him I didn't need them."

"Could I get them? So you can eat."

"Certainly. They're in that cubbyhole under the stairs down here. You'll have to move the hat rack over a little. Use what you need."

That guy really unloaded on Louise, Mari thought, as she tugged to get the bulging bag through the small door. *I'll pick out the colors I like, right here.* She chose two round gold pillows and four square ones, two brown and two dark green. *They'll go with the bedspread better than pink and red and purple.*

Mari listened to her radio and read until she was sleepy. *Even if Louise did ask me to watch TV there's not much that's worth seeing this afternoon.*

She felt her eyelids closing and let the book slide to the floor. When she woke up she began to think about what was ahead for her. *Since I left Castleton all the further I've seen is one day or the next meal. Now—well, do I want to stay here a long time? Everyone is good to me. And I'm not hungry or anything.* She turned over on her back and stared up at a brown spot on the ceiling made by a leak in the roof. She thought it looked a little like Abraham Lincoln.

She thought of Mr. Harrison, her history teacher. *When we got to the Civil War part of our books, we stayed there a long time. Then we had to hurry through the other chapters. I guess I never thought that running away meant I'd never get to go to school. But how can I? Part-time dishwashing would never pay for everything. But here I am. What else is there to do?*

She shook her head and blinked to keep tears from falling. *I'll call Patty and see if she can talk.*

Her cousin was alone. "Jay went up to his folks. But if we hear a click I'll hang up. Sometimes he checks on me on the party line."

"Can't you even talk to anyone?"

"Well, I can. But he asks a lot of questions. And there's hardly anyone Jay or his family thinks is as good as the Conleys. And when he says that I get mad. And when I get mad I cry. And I don't think that's good for Heidi."

"You think she notices, as little as she is?"

"Oh, yes, Mari. Her little face gets puckery. Babies know a lot more than most people realize. But don't think I don't want you to call me. Please don't give up on me."

"Don't worry. That won't happen. How about tomorrow afternoon? Is that a good time?"

"It is, especially this week. Jay's folks are going on a fishing trip for three or four days, down in Kentucky."

"You think they spy on you?"

"Some, yes. They didn't want Jay to marry me."

"Well, I'd better go. You give that little Heidi a hug for me."

I sure am glad I ran into Patty, Mari thought as she walked to the front door. *It seems like she needs someone as much as I do.* She watched two little boys riding tricycles along the sidewalk. One took his hands from the handlebars, held his arms straight out, and called, "Look at me. I'm a jet."

If he doesn't watch where he's going he'll be a plane that's crashed into a tree. She turned and looked around the archway, to see Louise's clock. *I'm always hunting ways to find out what time it is. Four-thirty. I guess it's not too early to get ready and walk over to the motel.*

She stopped at Emilie's door on the way out. "Need anything?"

"Are you going past the drugstore? Would it be out of your way to get a packet of envelopes? I'm catching up on my letter writing."

"It's on my way. How many?"

"They ususally have packages of twenty. That will be fine."

That's another thing that's changed. I don't get any mail, Mari thought. *I don't even expect any—not that I ever did get much. Just ads and cards from kids who have moved or are on vacation. But it was something to look forward to. But now—if no one knows where I am they can't write to me.*

The motel dining room was crowded. More people were seated at tables than Mari had seen there before. Two of the waitresses were new to Mari, but Liz was working. She hurried over to speak to Mari. "My goodness. You're all dressed up."

"I'm a paying customer this time."

"Well, sit down at one of my tables. And you don't have to order a full meal."

"Is that a rule?"

78

"Sort of—on Sunday nights. But Ellie's reasonable. She knows there are times when people don't need that much. We were hoping you'd come."

"You were? Why?"

"Oh, for no special reason. I hadn't seen your bright face for a while. Here's your menu."

But she said "we." Who did she mean? Why would anyone be hoping I'd come? Oh well, maybe they were just hoping I was all right—or something.

She decided to have chicken pie and peppermint ice cream with chocolate sauce. *That'll be all I really need.*

When Liz brought the food to the table she said, "Ellie hired a new cook yesterday—a real nice person. Before you leave I'd like for you to meet her."

"I didn't know she needed another cook," Mari said.

"Not another. This is a replacement. Hester had to quit because of high blood pressure or something."

As Mari picked up her napkin and looked at the plate she thought, *Someone's looking after me. They ususally only serve two biscuits to a person— not three.* The food tasted good and Mari took her time. She was in no hurry to get back.

She was reaching into her purse when Liz put a hand on her shoulder. "No tip, young lady. That's not allowed. Not among friends."

"How about that extra biscuit?" Mari whispered.

"You noticed?"

"I noticed. Thanks."

"Well, sometimes it pays to have a little influence with the cooks."

"How could you? She only came yesterday?"

"Who said I'm the one with the influence?"

What is she talking about? Mari wondered. *What's going on?*

As Liz led Mari to the cooks' area she noticed that everyone who was in the kitchen was watching her. They were all smiling, even the pan lady who almost never said a word.

"Where's the new cook?" Liz asked.

"Down here, scrubbing up a spill. Just a minute."

That sounds like Mom. But it couldn't be, Mari thought.

"Here's Mari, Mrs. Clayton," Liz said.

Mari felt her lower lip begin to quiver as she ran around the counter. *No matter why she's here. No matter what's going to happen, I'm glad.* "Oh, Mom, it's so good to see you!"

"I can hardly believe we're together again," her mother said as she held her close.

Mari felt her lower lip begin to quiver. "Oh, Mom, it's so good to see you!"

"I can hardly believe we're together again," her mother said as she held her close.

Chapter 11

I don't understand," Mari said as she reached for the Kleenex Liz handed aross the counter. "Are you working here?"

"I am. And I'd better finish up. Be sort of bad to get fired almost before I was hired. You wait on that stool or someplace and I'll get off in a half an hour or a little more."

"Did you know she was my mother before I came?" Mari said as she walked to the door with Liz.

"Yes. Ellie told us all this morning but I found out yesterday. When your mom was hired, Ellie called me for your telephone number, but I didn't know where you were staying."

"I never told anyone," Mari answered. "You mean she was here last night?"

"No. No. You'd have seen her. The way it was, the motel manager in Castleton called Ellie. He said he was losing a good cook and did she need one. But I've got to go! Another table just filled up. Oh, Mari. I'm so relieved that your mother's here. I've been so worried about you."

"You have?"

Mari walked back to the kitchen and sat on the high stool, hooking her heels over a rung. "Where— do you have a place to stay, Mom?"

Her mother took the stainless steel bowl of ground ham, boiled eggs, and pickles to the wide refrigerator with glass doors. "There, I've got a head start on tomorrow—at least on the ham salad. Now we can talk. We can start anyhow, while I change."

"I could stay here," her mother said as they went toward the small room which was the employee's lounge. "They offered me a room until I could get settled. But how about where you stay?"

"At Louise's. Sure. There's room. I don't think she'll care. She's real nice. And there are two beds." Then Mari added, "There's only one problem. You might get kicked if you scoot down too far."

"You're teasing. I can tell."

"Yep. I moved the furniture today, putting the beds together at a corner."

"It sounds like you were aiming to stay awhile."

Mari shook her head. "I didn't know what else to do. Not right now."

"Well, we've got a lot of talking to do," Bertie Clayton said. "But we don't have to do it all at once. I'll change out of this uniform and get my bags. Your room very far from here?"

"About two and a half blocks. Why?"

"Those suitcases are heavy. I stuffed them full. One's mostly your things."

"Sounds like *you're* aiming to stay awhile," Mari said.

"Could be," her mother said as they came out of the rest room. "At least until I decide what else to do. Ready to go?"

"Ready."

"Our belongings are at the front desk. Do you think we'll need a taxi?"

"A taxi! Mom, I've never ridden in a taxi in my whole life."

"Then we'll slurge. I drew a week's pay before I left Castleton. I had to buy a bus ticket but that didn't cost a whole lot. Besides, I'd been saving a little."

"It seems like you didn't have any trouble getting a job here."

"My goodness no. That's Mr. Julian's doing. As soon as I told him I knew you were here he put in the call."

"You knew where I was before you came?"

"That's exactly how it was. I came here *because* you're here. We'd better stand over where we can see that taxi pull up."

"But *how?* When? Who?"

"Well, the decision was made yesterday. When Mr. Harrison came to the motel and asked for me."

84

"Mr. Harrison? Mom! What does *he* have to do with all of this?"

"He saw you. There's the taxi. Can you lug that brown bag? It's not quite as big."

"Mom. I'm a big girl."

When the taxi pulled through the portico Mari began to laugh. "I'm so mixed up it's funny. I don't understand what's happened, why you decided to come, or what's going to come next. But I don't care. I'm willing to wait. As long as you're here, I'm plenty willing. Wait until I tell Patty this."

"Patty? Patty who?"

"Aunt Edna's Patty. Now *you're* mixed up. We'll probably talk half the night getting each other straightened out."

As the taxi pulled up to the curb Mari's mother said, "First things first. We have to get things set right with this Louise woman. Is that what you call her?"

"That's what she wants people to call her, instead of Lou. She's probably in the kitchen fixing Emilie's tray. She lives here, and has a broken ankle. Louise? You here?"

"Up here, Mari. I ate in Emilie's room tonight."

"You finished?"

"Yes. We—oh, you have a visitor."

"Yes. This is my mother, Bertie Clayton. She came here to work at the motel."

"Now isn't that nice. No wonder your eyes are sparkling. You're welcome to stay with your daughter, Mrs. Clayton, if you don't mind being crowded. If I had another room or a bigger one I'd offer it."

"No need to worry. I'm real glad to find a place—and to find Mari."

Louise looked at Mari and smiled. *Did she catch on that I'd run away? She doesn't look surprised.*

"You can bring your mother to meet Emilie after you get settled. It would be nice for us all to get acquainted. And before I quit jabbering—if you need a bigger place later on, we can get our heads together. I know this neighborhood like the palm of my hand."

"We may decide to do that," Mari's mother said as she set the heavy black bag down at the foot of one bed. "Once I get my feet under me solid."

"You're thinner, Mom. Have you been sick?"

"With worry. And shame."

"Shame?"

"Yes, because I didn't stand up to your dad."

"Mom, let's not talk about that tonight. That's what Patty and I did when we went to the shopping center. We just talked about pleasant things."

"You're right. The way I see it we can't get everything said that's on our minds. Not if I'm to get to work on time."

"You don't work from noon to after dinner?"

"No. Oh, I did today just to fill in. But the regular hours will be from seven until two. That way I can have evenings free."

"I go at noon and evenings."

"Not from now on," her mother said. "You're going to school, days."

"Here?"

"Yes. That's one thing I talked over with Mr. Harrison and—"

"Stop right there. Fill me in about him."

Her mother told Mari that the history teacher had been to some kind of a workshop in the city. He ate at the motel before starting back to Castleton and had seen Mari go through the dining room into the kitchen. "He came to see me at work instead of going to the principal or the attendance officer. He thinks a lot of you, honey."

"I know. But go on."

"There's not much more to say about that. I wanted to call over here but I was afraid you'd go someplace else if you found out I knew where you were. So I talked to Mr. Julian. He knew how rough it had been for me."

"Because of my running away?"

"No. For other reasons. But that's not a happy subject. It's your turn now. What's this about Edna's Patty?"

Mari told her mother how she had met her cousin and that Patty wasn't very happy about being married. "One good thing is that she has a little girl called Heidi. She's so cute."

"I never heard that Patty had a baby. Of course Edna never even mentions her anymore, so she couldn't have told me."

"Why would she be that set against Patty?"

"It's hard to say. In fact, it doesn't make any sense to me. Edna did the same thing herself. She ran off and married someone Mama didn't like. People are hard to figure out."

"Patty gets homesick sometimes," Mari said. "And lonely. She likes it that we can talk to each other on the telephone. So do I."

"We'll do what we can to help her. Do you think she'll want to see me?"

"Oh, Mom. I think Patty would be glad to see anyone from Castleton—and you more than most. You're like family."

"I hope—like family ought to be. Say, what time is it? Ten-thirty. We'd better get some sleep."

"I'm glad you have a watch," Mari said. "If I hadn't grabbed my little radio, the one you got with trading stamps, I wouldn't have had any idea of when to do what."

"We can do better than that. I brought my alarm clock. It's in the black bag. I'll dig it out. But let's leave the rest of the unpacking till another day."

"Where did you get those bags? I thought I took the only one we had."

"They're Mr. Julian's. I'll send them back by UPS. Don't you have a bathtub?"

Mari explained the arrangement. "You mean men room here too?"

"Yes, but I've never seen them. They aren't here much. No one explained why until last night. And I never asked."

"I was going to say it seems sort of funny to live in a place with other people and not know them. But it happens—even in families."

As her mother went down the hall the words *funny peculiar* came to her mind. Why did she and Patty begin using those words from an old cartoon show? Which one was it? Something about a boy who wore a beanie with a whirligig on top. *The name will come to me. That was when we were kids—and happier.*

"We didn't get to meet the lady across the hall," Mari's mother said after the alarm clock had been set for six-thirty and the lights were out. "It slipped my mind."

"They'll understand. Are you okay?"

"I'm fine, Mari. Better than I've been for days, or even years. It seems so peaceful here. Good night, honey."

"Good night, Mom."

Mari could hear the whir of tires and the hum of motors from passing cars. In between the clock kept time with little clicking ticks. "Mom, are you asleep?"

"No, not quite. Why?"

"I just thought of something—are you a runaway too?"

"Yes, I guess you could say so."

"Well, you're better off than I've been. You don't have to be scared someone's going to take you to a detention home."

"You were scared about that?"

"Yes, sometimes," Mari added. "If they do that."

"I'm sorry, honey. You don't need to worry about that anymore."

Chapter 12

The jangling alarm of the clock woke Mari the next morning. "Oh, I meant to shut that thing off," her mother said coming from the bathroom.

"You beat it up?"

"Yes. I'm looking forward to getting to work. Say! What do you do about breakfast?"

"Well, different things," Mari said as she yawned and stretched her arms above her head. "I keep some snacks in a drawer. Or I go to the drugstore or a quick food place."

"That's something we'll have to work out. We ought to find a bigger place where we can cook a little. Why don't you talk to Louise about that before you come to the motel. See what ideas she might have."

"I'll be there—at noon."

"*Today* at noon. Tomorrrow you'll be in school."

"Will it be somewhere close?"

"Where else? Here's where we are. Now I've got to go."

As Mari dressed and straightened the bedspreads she tried to picture how it would be to go to a different school. "I won't know anybody. I don't even know which school is near here. But I probably can't get out of going. I don't even want to get out of it, if I'm honest."

She ate the last of the apples and a chunk of cheese before going downstairs. *I'm supposed to talk to Louise and I want to call Patty—which should I do first?*

Emilie Wantz made the choice for Mari. She came from the direction of the kitchen. "You're up early and you don't have your cane," Mari said.

"No. I've leaned on it too long. I came downstairs on my own this morning to eat breakfast. Louise has something in mind for you and your mother."

"Mom's gone to work but she wants me to ask about a bigger place."

"That's what's on Lou's mind. You go on back."

"I've never really looked around in your kitchen before," Mari said as she walked into the sunlit room.

"Sit yourself down, and I'll go right ahead rolling out this pie dough."

"You're making apple pie, I see."

"Yes, help yourself to a slice or two of apples. I wanted to talk to your mother."

"That's what Emilie said."

Louise told Mari that she'd called two neighbors about apartments for rent. "Mrs. Spicuzza's sister has three rooms—the top floor of what used to be a three-car garage. It seems hard to believe anyone in this part of town could ever afford *three* automobiles."

"Do you know anything about the place?"

"Yes," Louise said as she sprinkled cinnamon over the apple slices. "A member of my Sunday school class lives in the downstairs. It's cozy and clean—not fancy, though."

"Do you think someone might get in ahead of us?"

"I can't say. But I did take it on myself to call Mrs. Spicuzza's sister to tell her I had a good prospect. Could you call your mother and give her this number?"

"Yes, I will right away. I think she'd want to know."

"Now I'm not trying to get rid of you. I hope you understand that," Louise said.

"I do. Mom's already said we need a place to cook."

"I can understand that. Here, use this phone."

Mari gave Ellie the message and telephone number and then she went to the telephone booth in the hall and called Patty. "Can you talk?"

"Yes, I can. And am I glad to hear your voice! Jay's going to enlist."

"He is? Does that upset you?"

"No, not too much. Except I don't know what I'm going to do. Not yet."

"Well, *I've* got some news! My mom's here." Mari told Patty what had happend, how she felt, and what might come next. "That's about all I can tell you so far. We haven't had much time to talk yet. But I'm going back to school."

"Oh, I'm so glad. Are you?"

"Yes—but I don't know anyone here."

"You will. I'll want to see Aunt Bertie and have her see Heidi."

"You will. I'll call back."

Mari thought of looking through the suitcases when she got back to the room. *I'd better not unpack, not if we might move. I'd like to peek at the one that has my things in it and see what Mom brought along. But I'd better get over to the motel.* She wore her checked dress. *Could be Mom will find out something about school, and I'll be going from there.*

As Mari walked to work she wished she'd asked Louise where the apartment was that they might rent. *I've got time and I'd sort of like to see how it looks.* She noticed things she'd never seen before. *It looks like a library up from the corner. And that must be a post office—a flag's flying. Why didn't I see these places before? Could be I was so scared someone would find out I'd run away from home I didn't notice much. Now I don't have to worry about that.*

A long red and silver bus edged around the corner and headed for the station two blocks away. *It seems like a long time since I leaned against a window and wondered if I'd find a place to stay.*

For the first time since she left Castleton, Mari let one question stay in her mind. *Did I know what I was really doing?* She knew what she'd said to herself over and over. *I'm not going to let Dad belt-whip me again. I'll run away first.*

As she crossed the motel parking lot she thought, *How'd I know he'd do it again? Probably because when he had too much to drink that's always what happened—if I got in his way.*

Ellie smiled at her from behind the cash register. "You look real happy this morning."

"Yes. I am."

"That's good. We'd worried about you."

"That's what Liz told me. Why?"

"We didn't want you to end up like so many runaways."

"You knew?" Mari said. "How could—"

"Oh, sweetie! We see so many. You were different. Not—well, not hopeless. You stood out from some of the others. I'd have given you that job even if you'd never heard of a dishwashing machine. I wanted to keep you from getting into the runaway stream—the muddy waters."

"I never thought you knew. I was so worried that you'd find out. And here I wasn't keeping anything from you at all. Say, I'm glad you gave Mom a job."

"We needed her," Ellie said as she reached for a customer's check.

Mari changed into her uniform and went to talk to her mother.

"Have you eaten?" Mari asked. "And did you call that lady about the apartment?"

94

"I haven't and I did. If you're not starved I could tell you what's what when you get off. A cook can't stop at noon."

"I can wait. See you."

The red-haired boy who washed pans at noon was leaning against the sink. "You're early," Mari said.

"I know. Ellie called me at school. She said she wanted to talk to me, if I could pedal my bike a little faster. About you."

"Me?"

"Yep. I'm going to take you to school."

"I'll bet you hate that—leading a new girl around. Say, I don't even know your name."

"I'm Kent. Kent Douglas. And it's not going to be such a bad deal to show *you* around."

"What's the name of the school? How far away is it?"

"Keystone, about five blocks south of here. Think you can make it? Or do you want me to give you a ride on the handlebars?"

"I'll walk, thank you. Out of pity for you."

"Okay. I'll be at the office door at two-fifteen. That's the break between periods."

Mari didn't say much while she ate lunch, for two reasons. She didn't have much time and her mother had a lot to say about several things. "First, I want to tell you we can see that apartment at four. Do you suppose you'll be through at the school by then?"

"Why wouldn't I? Everyone will probably be gone before then. Did she say how much it will cost?"

"No, we'll have to think about that later."

"This lasagna is really delicious," Mari said.

"They must have a good cook here."

"Think so, do you?"

"I called Patty," Mari said as she ate her peach Jello. "She wants to see you. And she had some news. Jay's enlisting in something."

"The way you say his name I gather you don't like him."

"I never even saw him but I don't like him—because of the way he treats Patty."

"It sounds like you and I are down on men."

"Not all of them, I guess."

"Oh, no. I wouldn't have this job if Mr. Julian hadn't put in a good word for me. And I wouldn't have found you *and* the job if it hadn't been for Mr. Harrison."

"I have to go, Mom. But I can't keep still about something any longer. I stole money from you. I'm sorry. Did you know? I'll pay it back from my wages."

"I knew," Mari's mother said as she reached over and squeezed her hand. "What did you do with it?"

"Well, it went for a bus ticket and a week's room rent, and a Twinkie and two batteries—"

"I didn't mean for you to account for every single penny. I'm just grateful you could *pay* for a room. You don't need to pay me back."

"Patty said that you'd feel like that."

"Sometimes you young people know us adults better than we think. Now you'd better scoot."

Mari brushed her hair until it crackled with electricity. Then she smoothed the fly-away hairs with the palms of her hands. Her heart beat faster as she walked into Keystone High School. The halls

96

echoed with the voices of students rushing from one class to another.

"All visitors are to report to the office," she heard someone behind her say and turned to see Kent. "I was watching for you. Turn left here. We go to one of the counselors. I already asked."

Mari smiled her thanks.

"This is Mari Clayton," Kent said as they went through a door with frosted glass. "I'll leave you in his hands—oh, I slipped up, this is Mr. Donally. See you, Mari."

I don't know how I'll feel about having a man for a counselor. At Castleton we only had Miss Lederer, Mari thought.

"Mary, sit down, please," the tall man said as he pushed his tan-rimmed glasses to the bridge of his nose.

I know he's thinking M-a-r-y, she thought. "My name's really Marian," she said. "That's the way it is on the records at Castleton."

"Your records are on the way. Dorah Lederer called."

"You know her?"

"Yes. And Dave Harrison over there is a friend of mine. We taught together. He called me last night at home and asked us to take good care of you."

Mari looked at the counselor through a mist. *Mr. Harrison's a really great teacher. But I never expected him to put himself out for me like that.*

"Can you tell me what classes you were in so we can assign you to the right ones here? If we have any questions after the records come we'll get in touch."

"Is that all there is to it—to changing schools?"

Mr. Donally smiled, "Were you afraid we'd give you exams?"

"I just didn't know."

"There *is* one thing. I'll need an address."

"We may move, but right now we're on Keystone the other way." Mari wrote the house number on a file card before leaving. Then she hurried toward Louise's. *That was a lot easier than I thought. There was no need to be so scared.*

As she waited for a traffic signal to change from red to green she thought about Buffy and her group. Did they want to run away from school? Was everything a bad scene to them? Maybe they'd like to go back to school too if they knew how to work it out. She shook her head. *I can't solve their problems for them, I guess. I'm barely getting my own straightened out.*

Chapter 13

Mari's mother was waiting in a green slatted porch swing. "I never noticed that before," Mari said from the sidewalk.

"That's because it wasn't here," her mother said. "I helped hang it. Louise said she always had trouble moving it alone. But she didn't want winter winds banging it against the house."

"It seems like spring's really here," Mari said as they headed east.

"Yes. Of course we can still have a few cool days. I remember once when I was your age the redbud trees were already in bloom, when a soft snow came. The next morning they looked so pretty, like they were decorated with bits of sparkly cotton on the lavendar and pink sprays."

"Wasn't it hard on the trees?"

"They survived. Oh, here's the house. Louise said it had a brick railing on the porch."

A short lady with shining black hair came to the door. "You're Lou's friends," she said. "Let me get my keys and we'll go around back."

Mari followed her mother and the person she knew only as Mrs. Spicuzza's sister to the back of the lot. "I've thought a dozen times of moving out here myself. But I couldn't put seven rooms in three, and the very thought of sorting between what to take and what to leave kept me where I am. There, go right in. Look around and bring the key back."

They faced open shelves that made a kind of entrance hall, then walked around them to a room that took up half the space.

"The furniture's pretty nice," Mari said. "Two couches."

"One looks like a sofa bed," her mother said. "Louise told me that this woman—I meant to ask her first name—isn't strapped for money and likes to change furniture. What she gets tired of she uses to help furnish another apartment. She owns another house with four apartments in it."

Mari went ahead of her mother. "Here's the kitchen."

"I see it's good-sized. And that's the bathroom. The bedroom's probably in front."

Mari looked out all the windows while her

100

mother opened closet doors and cabinet drawers. "You like it, don't you, Mom?"

"Yes. It's better'n what I had. A long ways better. How about you?"

"I like it, too. It seems—as Louise says—cozy. Do you suppose it costs too much?"

"That's what I have to find out. But I tell you something, honey. I'd be willing to skimp on a lot of other things to get this. Already I feel—well, at home."

"You said you had some money saved."

"That's true. Long before you left I had it in my mind to rent a place for us two—for a while anyway."

"You were thinking of leaving Dad?"

"Yes, in a way. Not divorce. At least not at first. Just to give him a chance to find out if he wanted to wean himself from the bottle. But we'd better find out what the rent is."

As her mother locked the door Mari said, "I can still pay you back the twenty I owe you. And I can keep on working evenings and some on weekends. Wouldn't that help?"

"It certainly would."

Fifteen mintues later they left for Louise's with a key to the upstairs apartment. "I don't look at things like most owners," Mrs. Spicuzza's sister said. "I don't advertise, and I don't charge everyone the same. I tell myself, 'Now, Rosa, don't go against your hunches. You've always had a feel for picking good renters.'"

At least we know her first name's Rosa, Mari thought.

"Are you sure it's what you want?" Mari's mother asked again.

Mari nodded. "Sure. And it's close to the motel and school."

She remembered being surprised when her mother gave Rosa ninety dollars for the first month's rent and thinking, *I didn't know she'd saved that much. And there's some left.*

"You think it was safe to carry so much around?" Mari asked as they walked.

"No, but I didn't know what else to do with it. I left some more—well, not very much—in the savings account at home. But I don't know who'd cash a check for me away from home."

"Louise would , or Ellie."

"Probably, but I didn't know I was going to run into people like them. Sometimes we get to thinking there's no kindness in big cities."

"When are we going to move?"

"I was turning that over in my mind while Mrs. DeLand was writing out the receipt."

"How'd you know her last name?" Mari asked.

"It's on the receipt. You'll have to go to work before long. But I could move enough to tide us over until tomorrow."

"You mean we could stay there tonight?"

"Why not? The rent's paid."

"It's paid two places. We could stay at either."

"Two places to lay our heads."

"What does that mean?"

"Oh, it's something the young minister said when I went to talk to him about your father's drinking— and about you being away."

"What minister?"

"It's kind of a long story," her mother said. "We'll get into that later. Now you come to Louise's first and see if there's anything you should bring over."

I don't remember when things ever seemed so great, Mari thought as she slipped into her tan and cream uniform. *I wish Liz was working so I could tell her about the apartment. Maybe she could come visit us sometime.* Later she was surprised when Ellie walked into the kitchen. "You been here all day?" Mari asked her.

"No, I was home a few hours. But the night cashier wanted to go to a wedding."

"I have to get to work—but I'm bursting to tell someone. Mom,—we—found an apartment."

"Well, wonderful. And I hear you're going back to school."

"Tomorrow."

"We'll get together if you want to work, and talk about new hours."

"Oh, I will—want to, I mean."

Mari took time to eat her evening meal. "I don't know what I'll do for food tonight if I don't. There wouldn't be any at the apartment yet."

Louise was watching television but she got up and turned the knob when Mari walked into the hall. "We have our work cut out for us." she said. "Your mother left one bag for us to move."

"We?" Mari said. "I can carry *one.*"

"I know. But I gathered up a few more things— with Emilie's help. And I'd sort of like to see you settled in."

"That's nice."

103

"We'll take turns with the bag. It's heavier than this box of goodies."

"What's in there?"

"Oh, a kind of housewarming present—an apple pie and a glass of grape jelly. And Emilie had me get a loaf of bread from the bake shop and a carton of ham salad. We figured you might want to do some snacking."

"I guess I'll never be able to tell you how I feel about you and Emilie. You've been so good to me, and now to Mom too."

"No need for thanking us. Are you ready?"

"Yes—but wait one minute. I should call Patty."

"Your cousin? Your mother talked to her a long time. She saw where you had jotted Patty's number on the directory."

"Then Patty knows where we'll be?"

"Yes, she does. Something was said about her spending a day with you, when it's your mother's day off."

"Great."

It was dark by the time they came to the wooden steps that led up to the apartment. "The lights are on downstairs too. Does your friend still live there?"

"Yes. I thought I might check on her while I'm over this way."

"Here, let me take that," Mari's mother said as she opened the door.

"This looks real—"

"Cozy," Mari said.

"You're right," Louise agreed. "It looks like you're already settled."

"Well, there wasn't much to do. I put out some of our things, Mari's music box and a few of her books—the ones I saw her read over and over."

"And I see your crystal candlestick and the little silver bell."

"Yes. I've kept them all these years since we divided up Mama's things. I couldn't bear to leave them—to get broken maybe."

"Louise and Emilie fixed some things for us," Mari said.

"My lands! You didn't have to do that."

"No, we didn't."

When Louise said she had to go, Mari's mother said, "Now you come back. I tell you, I'll never forget how you took care of Mari."

"That wasn't any chore," Louise said. "You'll stop by to see me now and then, I hope."

"We'll stop by," Mari answered. She shut the door and said, "I can't wait any longer to see what else you packed for me besides the books."

"Take the suitcase back to the bedroom."

"But that should be your room. I can sleep on the couch."

"Please, Mari," her mother said, "I'd rather sleep here."

Mari saw tears in her mother's eyes. "Did I say something wrong?"

"No, but I've hidden the pain and suffering of my life with your father behind a bedroom door so many many times. I've tried to keep you from seeing, from hurting. But I didn't get that done, did I? Not always anyways."

"Don't cry, Mom. Don't think about the bad.

Things are beginning to look a lot better, aren't they?"

"Yes. But the time has to come when I can put into words how bad I feel about things. Then we can go on."

"We're going on now, Mom. How about a piece of Louise's apple pie before we go to bed? Are there any dishes?"

"There are—and some of anything else we'll really need. But I thought you were going to unpack."

"That's right. The pie can wait."

It was nearly ten o'clock before Mari found places for the sweaters and shorts and pleated skirts and her tan gabardine coat. She took her autograph book and the picture of her friend Lois Ann to the shelves at the front entrance. "Did you see Lois Ann after I left?"

"Yes, a couple of times. Once at home—and she came by the motel to ask if I'd heard from you."

"Does she know now—where I am?"

"No. I wanted to tell her but I couldn't make up my mind what was best."

"You mean Dad might try to pump her."

"Yes. What do you think?"

"I don't know. I'd like for her to know where we are, but I don't want Dad coming and finding us. Do you think he'd think of us being here?"

"No, he'd never believe I had the nerve to go to a big city. And maybe there's no use to worry. He might not even look. I'm not sure he cares that much. Now, I'm ready for apple pie."

"So am I."

Chapter 14

Mari didn't hear the alarm clock the next morning, and didn't know it was another day until her mother called, "Time to get ready for school." She said it out loud, not in a whisper like she used to do at home to keep from making Dad mad or waking him up.

Mari lay still for a while. *I wish I didn't keep thinking about Dad. It seems like I'd be glad to forget all about him. But after all, he is my father. If someone could help him quit drinking, he'd probably be a good man.*

She decided to wear the white sweater with her

brown skirt. *I'll give that black-and-white-checked dress a rest—not that I have such a great choice.*

"Think you can make out with toast and jelly and tea? Louise tucked a half-dozen tea bags and some sugar cubes in the box."

"I'll bet the cubes were Emilie's idea. I saw some in her room in a square glass jar."

As they ate at the drop-leaf table, Mari's mother talked about what they needed to buy. "Food for one thing. I've started a list. And shampoo. I was out. And it wouldn't hurt if you had another outfit. Do you know where we can buy all this?"

"All but the food. I know about the Jiffy Market but it's not a very big place."

"Well, I'll call Louise. And if you want to go along shopping with me, I'll stay at the motel until you come from school. That will save a few blocks' walk for you. Are you dreading today, honey?"

"A little," Mari said. "I mean, I don't know anyone except Kent and the counselor. I don't know if I'm afraid everyone will stare at me or that they might not know I'm around."

The closer Mari came to the large tan brick building, the slower she walked. The words, "Here I come—ready or not," came to her mind. As she started up the steps, Kent Douglas came to meet her. He told her he thought she'd gone in another door.

"I don't even know which the right door is. But you didn't have to worry."

"Who's worried? I'll show you where your classes are and the cafeteria. Or will you work at noon?"

"No, just evenings and some on weekends. I don't

108

know how much." As they went to the end of the long hall Mari asked, "Did you know I was a runaway?" The words came out almost without thinking.

"Sure. So what? This is where you'll be first, for English, and if we hurry we can make it back here before the bell." Mari didn't talk as they walked because she was trying to memorize the location of the rooms. When they arrived back at the English room Kent handed her a piece of scrap paper. "Here's the room numbers and your teacher's names."

"Oh, thanks! That will help."

"Thank Mr. Donally. Say, Nancy! Want to shepherd a new member of the flock? Mari—with an i—Clayton. This is Nancy Mattingly."

"Hi, Mari," the girl with brown eyes and honey hair said. "Isn't he something! A person'd think the twenty-third psalm was his dictionary—words from it keep popping up in his talk. Come along."

"Why?" Mari asked. "Why does he talk like that?"

"Because he *is* like that. He's for real. You'll find out if you know him long enough. I'll introduce you to the teacher when she comes in."

"Are seats assigned?"

"Not unless someone gets out of line. Then *they're* moved."

By the end of the day Mari's uneasiness about going to a new school was almost gone. "Keystone kids don't seem much different from those in Castleton. There are all kinds."

She had gone to the cafeteria alone and was putting the gray plastic tray on a corner table when

Nancy came toward her. "Come eat with us over here. There's a chair." The other three girls were friendly and didn't ask many questions. One said she'd seen Mari with Kent and another wanted to know where she'd met him. The third asked where she'd come from.

But that's all they asked, Mari had thought as she went into the social studies room. She glanced at the paper. *Mr. Rust. Well, he doesn't know it, but this teacher has to be really good if this class is going to be as interesting as Mr. Harrison made his.*

I don't think it's going to be so bad here, Mari thought as she went to meet her mother. *But I probably won't find a friend like Lois Ann.* She saw her mother sitting at the wide window of the motel lobby, and saw her get up and start toward the door.

I have a kind of map," her mother explained."Louise told me a good place to buy groceries and about a shopping center. Liz drew me a map. She's the nicest person! The bus stop—it's which way?"

"The bus to the shopping center? It's this way."

"You've been there?"

"A couple of times."

Mari's mother shook her head. "It scares me to think of you wandering around in a strange city—alone."

"It scared me too, Mom."

As they got off the bus Mari hoped she wouldn't run into Buffy and her group, or that they wouldn't see her. *I don't think Mom will like the way they look.*

"Have you been thinking of what you might like to buy in the way of clothes?"

"A little," Mari said. "The school colors are red and white. And jumpers are *in* over here."

"A red jumper. That would match with things you have. Let's look."

They'd found a corduroy jumper with a silver ring on the zipper and had stopped for a pineapple julep when Mari saw Buffy coming toward her. *She looks a mess, even worse than usual. Her hair's oily and she doesn't even have sandals on today.*

"Hey, Castleton. You've not been around."

"No, I'm in school."

"Wow! Trapped again, huh?"

"No, I'm in school. I like it. Come on, Mom. Let's go."

"Who in the world? How do you know—"

"I don't. Not too well. I'll explain on the bus. We don't have that much time."

After Mari explained to her mother that Buffy had remembered seeing her in the Candy Box and had come up to her in the mall she said, "They wanted me to join up."

"Would you? How do they live?"

"Mom, I don't think you even want to think about how they live. I don't know it all—just enough to be scared at the thought of going their way. Living all together, getting money any way they can. And I mean *any* way."

"Oh, honey. Did you ever think of doing that?"

"No, not yet. But sometimes I worried about what I would do if I ran out of money."

"You didn't think of coming home at *all?*"

111

"Oh, yes. Then I'd imagine how hard Dad would be on me. It's not easy to go back, I guess. That one night, when the Peace of Mind people called you, was the worst. I cried a lot."

"The Peace of Mind people? Honey, what are you talking about?"

"Didn't they call? The night before you came here. The people who keep saying a million beds won't be slept in tonight."

"You called them?"

"Yes. It was late. I slipped downstairs and asked them to tell you I was okay."

"Let's see—oh, I didn't stay at home that night. Your father—well, he was worse than usual. I stayed at the motel. I left from there. You wanted me to know where you were?"

"No, they don't tell that. Just that I was okay and not doing anything bad."

"Oh, Mari, the mistakes I've made. But I guess I can't do my confessing to you now like I did to that minister. Here's where we get off. The market's two blocks that way. You going straight to work?"

"Yes. I'll eat first. See you."

As Mari walked she put some of the things her mother had said together. *Like hiding in the bedroom to keep me from being hurt. Maybe she had it a lot harder than I ever knew. But what did she mean about confessing to a minister? I didn't know she knew any. I guess people don't always know each other even if they live in the same house.*

Mari ate ham and escalloped potatoes while listening to the sounds of the dining room, the clink of silverware, the murmur of voices. She was reaching for the dish of fruit salad when Kent Douglas came to the table. "What are you doing here?"

"I'm talking to you. Any objections?"

"No, why?"

"Why what?"

"Why should I object?"

"That would be for you to know and me to find out. But that's enough of that kind of talk. I wanted to ask you if you'd like to join a group I'm in—at least visit once."

"What kind of a group?"

"Well, it meets in a church, but you don't have to join it. We do things like go to nursing homes and write letters for people or make telephone calls. Sometimes we play with the children."

"Kids in *nursing homes?*"

"In some places. Little ones who have lots of problems. Are you interested?"

"Yes, I've never done anything like that but it sounds okay."

"We'll go Sunday afternoon at two. Where do you live?"

"Up Keystone at the back of 1534. But I'd better find out when I'm going to work before I say for sure."

"No problem. I'll come by tomorrow."

Does he like me or is he just being kind? I wonder if Nancy belongs to this bunch? I never did go with a church group. I guess it won't hurt to give it a try. I'm sure they won't be like Buffy's groupies. Maybe even Buffy would be nice if she left her gang and found better friends.

When Mari went to the kitchen the evening cook said, "Ellie wants you to call her before you leave."

"Do you know why?"

"About weekend hours. She's made a schedule."

"Okay, thanks."

Mari hummed as she racked and stacked dishes. *I really have great vibes,* she thought. *A good place to live. School not so bad. Mom here. And Kent and Nancy and a job. That all adds up to a lot of good.*

She called Ellie and agreed to the idea of working four hours on Saturday and having Sunday off. "Now, the next weekend you'll both have Saturday off. I've already talked this over with your mother."

Mari hurried home, stopping only long enough to talk to Louise and Emilie, to tell them she thought school was going to be okay. "Now you come see us. Can you walk that far, Emilie?"

"I can and I will, and that's a promise."

"We're going to have company," Mari's mother said as she met her at the door.

"You mean Emilie and Louise?"

"No. Not that *they* wouldn't be welcome. It's Patty and her baby—what's the little one's name?"

"Heidi. When are they coming?"

"Sunday for dinner. I called on the way home."

"Great," Mari said. "Kent asked me to go with a group from a church at two. But I don't have to."

"No. You go ahead with your plans. Patty's coming in early and may be ready to leave by then. You *should* get acquainted with your new friends. Besides, Patty and I have a lot of catching up to do—like you and me."

"Right, Mom."

Chapter 15

The next few days gave Mari the feeling that she was living in a new world. *It's like I have a real home for the first time,* she thought as she left school Friday afternoon. *I don't dread going in the door and I don't have to think about how my dad's going to treat me.* She went home from school before going to work, not caring that it meant she had to walk several more blocks.

One evening they had time to go to the laundromat together and Mari folded some clothes while her mother tried operating the ironer.

"When I see how we come out after I put aside

rent money I'll shop for an iron," her mother said.

"Do you suppose we'll ever have a TV?" Mari asked as they carried the clean clothes back to the apartment, some on hangers, the rest in a cardboard box.

"Didn't I tell you?" her mother said. "Rosa is thinking about getting a new one with a bigger screen. She's going to ask what they'd give her as a trade-in. Then she might offer it to us."

"I'll help pay, Mom."

"We'll see."

As Mari hurried up the steps the next day she recognized a voice she'd heard many times before. *I know that commercial.* She skipped three of the six top steps and saw the portable television. "Mom. You did it. Where are you?" When no answer came she went to the kitchen and found a note under the peanut-butter jar.*That's one thing that's like Castleton. She always held messages down like this.* "At Rosa's. Painting. Stop on way to work. Enjoy yourself."

Mari smiled as she spread a slice of bread with butter and some of Louise's grape jelly. *I think Mom knew she was going to get this TV. She wanted it to be a surprise.* She kicked off her shoes, stretched out on one of the couches, and started to watch a soap opera. *I don't know what's going on. It's been so long. And that man wasn't even on this show. He died on another channel.* She switched to a game show and decided she'd better not start to get involved in watching it. *I have to get to work and I want to give myself time to find out what Mom's painting—and why.*

116

Mrs. DeLand met Mari at the door. "Looking for your mother? She's in here. You want to know what she's up to, huh?"

She doesn't give me a chance to answer, Mari thought. *She just hurries on to another question.*

"Here's your girl," Rosa said. "She came to check up on you."

"I expected you, honey," Bertie Clayton said from a stepladder in the corner of the room. Her head was wrapped in paper towels and she held a roller, soaked in pale blue. "Were you surprised?"

Mari nodded and smiled. "I sure was. Thanks, Mom. Is this how you're paying for it?"

"Yes. We got it all worked out. Rosa ordered new carpet for in here. It won't be in for two weeks or more. So I can do this job a little at a time."

"You going to work late?"

"No, this wall should be covered before you're off work. Then I'll fix me a bite to eat."

"I'll be seeing you. Watch it."

The evening cashier picked up an envelope and waved it as Mari walked through the dining room. "Payday," she said. "Forget?"

"No," Mari said, "but I hadn't thought about it for a few hours." As she went to the rest room she thought, *Things sure have changed in a hurry. Just a week ago I could hardly wait until I got paid. Now I have other things to think about.*

I'd like to take Mom a surprise—one that doesn't cost a lot, Mari thought as she ate, trying to remember what she'd noticed in the stores in the neighborhood. *She doesn't wear jewelry, except her cameo and the wide bracelet that was Grandma's.*

For some reason she remembered the fern in Louise's living room.

Mom likes plants. She says it's a pleasure to keep them growing. Do they have plants in drugstores or in the Jiffy Market?

As she walked home she stopped at every corner and looked up streets she hadn't been on yet. She almost missed seeing a small greenhouse at the side of a building which had a shoe repair sign out front.

She was a little surprised to find it open and told this to the slender man who came from the back.

"It's not unusual for me to be here till ten or so," he said. "It rests me to work at repotting and rooting plants. What do you have in mind, young lady?"

"A present for my mother. I don't know much about plants except cactuses and African violets. Mom likes things that vine."

"How about this?" the man said as he picked up a pot from which green leaves tinged with white trailed over the sides. "This is Swedish ivy."

"That's fine." She didn't care how much it cost and felt good as she put two dollars and fifty cents in the hands of the greenhouse owner. "Mom will be glad to know about this place."

"Fine and dandy. If I'm not here I'll be next door, like as not."

"I brought *you* something," Mari said as she went to the kitchen. "What are you doing now?"

"Stirring up a cake for Sunday, for when Patty

"How about this?" the man said as he picked up a pot from which green leaves tinged with white trailed over the sides. "This is Swedish ivy."

comes. Oh, my goodness! what a healthy-looking ivy. Thank you, Mari. I think I'll put it—let's see—there are so many good places here, so much sunlight. Try it on the end table by the short sofa."

"I thought you'd be tired."

"Well, I am. But it's a good kind of weariness with no worries mixed up in it. Not many, anyway."

"What does that mean?"

"Wait until I slide these pans in the oven," her mother said. "I think it's time I got some things said and out of the way."

Mari felt a little uneasy. *I guess I don't want a good thing messed up. But that's probably how Mom feels too.*

"What I meant by not much worry is that I can't help thinking about what's happening to your father. I keep wondering if the minister got to him at all."

"You never explained how you know him—the minister."

Bertie sat down in the swivel chair and talked for nearly ten minutes. She explained that two days after Mari ran away she was afraid to be in the house because Mari's father was drunk most of the time. "I knew he was being hard on himself and was afraid he was going to be even harder on me. More than I could bear.

"I took a long walk, not knowing or caring where I went. After what must have been an hour I saw the light shining on the steeple of the new church. You know the one over on Twelfth Street. I must have gone in circles—only a person can't go in

120

circles when they're walking around squares. Anyway, I'd headed myself back toward home."

She reached up and locked her hands behind her head. "Without even thinking, *I'm going into that church*, that's what I did. There was a light, a soft one up in front, and I sat down and began to cry. I couldn't seem to stop. Then someone from across the middle aisle said, 'Can I help?' "

"Who was it ?"

"The minister, the one I've mentioned. His name's Richard Amory. He doesn't want people to call him Reverend. He asked me what my burden was. And he listened—really listened. He didn't say a word until I said that was all."

"Did he put you down because of the mess in our family?"

"Oh, no. He said the most important thing was to find you before any harm came to you. He told me he'd begin praying about that."

"Was that *all?* Did he think that would help?"

"Something worked. Two days later Mr. Harrison came to see me. Who am I to say there's not a connection?"

"What about Dad? Didn't he want to pray for him?"

"I don't know. But he did say your father would have to admit he needed help, like I was doing by being in the church. But Richard is going to try to reach him through a group of people that used to drink too much."

"AA's."

"You know about them?"

"Yes, one talked to our health class," Mari said.

121

"Mom, do you think Dad will listen?"

"I don't know, Mari. I don't know. Wait until I take that cake out of the oven," she said, heading for the stove. "But I'm sure about this," she said as she came back, "I wasn't helping him by being there. He kept getting worse. Maybe this way he'll at least have a chance to come to his senses and turn around and go another way."

"I guess it's been a lot harder on you than I realized."

"It's like I said before. I tried to hide my hurts. Sometimes I felt like I was climbing a mountain. But almost every time I went up two steps, I'd slide back three. It was like that until I began to take in ironings. You might say I held my ground then. And going to the motel and being able to save some money—I was making progress. But one thing I didn't count on was you running away."

"But that's over. I'm here. You're here. I think things are great. Don't you?"

"They surely are. I thank the Lord. I truly thank Him. But there's another thing I have to get cleared up. Was everything at home *bad?* Didn't I give—"

"Oh, no, Mom, not everything. I thought about this before you came here. I mean the reason I did such a dumb thing. I think I talked myself into it. Like after Dad beat me the last time. I said over and over that he'd never do that to me again, that I'd run away first. Besides, a lot of girls talk about running away, but usually they don't mean it. Like Lois Ann. Did she tell you?"

"She told me."

"Anyway, I could see Dad was getting worse—

122

drinking more. And it was a little thing that de-cided me. I heard his whiskey talk after you stood up to him that last morning. Remember? He wanted money from you."

"I know. But there's something I don't think you realize. When I did stand firm for something and for you—and Mari, I did sometimes—he was al-ways harder on you."

"Why?"

"Because. That's the way he could hurt me most."

"I never thought—oh, Mom. I'm glad we're here."

"So am I. Probably I should have left long ago. But things could have turned out much worse. Do you think you *would* have gone to living like Buffy before you'd have come back home?"

"No, I don't see how I could. What do you think will happen—about Dad?"

"I don't know. It's up to him now. As far as I can see all we need to do now is go on like we are."

"Up the mountain, huh?"

"In a way. Now, I'd better put the icing on the cake."

"Do you feel better?"

"So much better, honey. Thanks for under-standing."

Chapter **16**

A drumming sound woke Mari the next morning. She blinked. *That's rain on the roof. It kind of rumbles and patters at the same time.* She pulled the blanket up over her shoulders after turning to face the window. The trees were below her except the top of one her mother called a Lombardy poplar. Its tip was a green steeple and Mari could see the wings of a bird fluttering with the swaying of the wind. *Having a little trouble holding onto your perch, little bird?* she thought.

She raised her head and looked toward the living room. *Mom's shut the door. Probably didn't want to wake me with whatever she's doing.*

"What's on this early in the morning?" she said as she sat down beside her mother on the couch. "Oh, a church program."

"Yes. Emilie says she watches it."

"The flowers sure are pretty," Mari said.

"Yes, and during the singing they zoom in on a fountain and a statue of Jesus, the Good Shepherd, with some sheep."

Mari thought of Kent Douglas and what Nancy said about the Bible being his dictionary. *Do what all people think and believe show up in their talk?*

"I'm going to ask Louise about her church," Mari's mother said when the program was over. "For one thing it doesn't seem right to take help from Richard Amory and not give back thanks in some way. Besides, I need something more in my life." Then she reached over and cupped Mari's face in her hands. "God loves you and so do I."

That's what that preacher said, Mari thought.

"Well, I'd better get to cooking breakfast and then some Sunday dinner. You know, it seems nice to be getting a meal for company. It's been a long time. My mother had someone almost every Sunday. She said it was the brightest day of the week."

"This one isn't so bright, outside anyway."

"I know. But we're snug. And even if we need to go out it's like Mother said, 'I won't melt. I'm neither sugar nor salt nor nobody's honey.'"

"Your mother must have had a lot of things she said over and over."

"She certainly did. If you ask me to repeat all of them, I probably couldn't think of more than two or three. But every so often one pops up from somewhere, and fits into what I'm saying."

Mari had eaten oatmeal and toast with jelly, made her bed, and helped with the dishes by nine o'clock. "If you don't have anything for me to do I'll watch for Patty. I'll help her up the stairs with Heidi."

"You do that," her mother said. "I'll brown this chicken, then put it in the oven for slow tenderizing."

Several cars went both ways on Keystone Avenue, but most of the people who walked were going in one direction. *There's probably a church down there somewhere—Louise's maybe.* She thought about Nancy Mattingly and hoped she'd be in the church group. *I never thought I'd have a friend like Lois Ann, but I guess a person could find a close friend most anywhere.*

She saw the yellow truck pull up to the curb. "There's Patty, Mom."

"Hadn't you better get a scarf or jacket?" her mother called.

"Mom. *I'm* neither sugar nor salt nor nobody's honey."

Heidi held out her arms to Mari. "I think she remembers me."

"I've been telling her we were going to see Mari. I brought you some of Mrs. Dane's magazines. She doesn't want them back."

"Great."

The girls blotted their shoes on a small mat as Mari's mother said, "Let's see if this little girl will come to her Great-Aunt Bertie."

126

"*Great*-aunt?" Mari said.

"That's what I am."

"That's what you are to me," Patty said. "A *great* aunt. It's so good to see you."

The three of them visited in the living room for over two hours. Heidi sat on the floor and played with a bag of blocks and the silver bell. Patty had asked, "Aren't you afraid she'll break it?"

"No, it's stood the test. You and Mari both played with it and your little brother, while he was alive."

"Poor Mama. I don't think she ever got over losing Eddie. She just got more and more bitter against life."

"Yes, it's a shame," Bertie Clayton said.

No one spoke for a few minutes. Heidi tumbled four blocks she'd stacked and the raindrops clicked against the south window. "Did Mama ever mention me at all?" Patty asked.

"No, honey. Not to me. But we didn't talk as often as we used to."

"Does she know where *you* are?" Patty asked.

"No. But I'll write to her when the time seems right. And is it all right if I say we're together? I'm itching to tell her about your little girl."

"It's okay," Patty said. "But I don't expect her to change."

"Let's not give up on Edna yet. Could be loneliness will move her to reach out. Now, what's this I hear about your husband going to the Army?"

"It's the Navy," Patty said, "and he's already gone."

"Do you plan to stay out there near his parents?"

"For now." Patty told them that she and Jay had

talked for a whole afternoon the day before he left. "His folks took him to the airport at six." She said they hadn't talked that much for months and that Jay had admitted he resented the fact that he felt compelled to get married. "We were both too young to know what we were getting into," Patty said.

"The same thing is true for so many others," Mari's mother said, "for a long time back."

"Anyway, we're not going to get a divorce. I never wanted one. I mean if Jay hadn't been important to me, well, we wouldn't be married at all. I wouldn't have run away with just anyone."

She said that some of Jay's pay would be sent to her and that he had the truck repaired for her before he left. "Since the mobile home's paid for and on his folk's land I won't have any rent."

"Will they look out for you?" Mari's mother asked.

"Too much so," Patty said. "Like I told Mari. But Jay said I should get a private telephone line if I can or get hooked up to a different party line. That will help."

"Well," Mari's mother said, "I must put the finishing touches on our dinner."

As they ate they made plans for the next weekend. Patty said she'd come and get them and they could stay at her place all day—or even longer. "I have a sofa bed, but you'd probably need to be back early to go to work."

"I would, " Bertie Clayton said. "But Mari could stay. We'll work that out."

As Mari scooped ice cream onto saucers alongside a wedge of chocolate cake she heard Patty ask, "Do you think Uncle Bud will go to AA like you said on the phone?"

"I don't know. Richard Amory—he's the minister—said he'd let me know if Marion turns over a new leaf. But it can't be easy for him either to admit he needs help or to stick with it."

"That's a good thing about Jay. He went fishing and hunting more than I thought we could afford. But he didn't drink. He doesn't really hurt me, except with words."

By the time Heidi woke from her afternoon nap, Patty was ready to go. "Jay said he'd call at three to let me know his address and tell me when I'd get a check—if he can find out."

"If you need money, I can help," Mari's mother said. "Would you tell me?"

"Yes, Aunt Bertie, I would. Mainly because I know you'd feel terrible if I didn't. Am I right?"

"You're right."

Mari and her mother stood on the sidewalk until the yellow pickup truck was out of sight. "She looks a lot better," Mari said.

"Does she? Of course I've not seen her for a while, but she seemed so worn—older."

"But not as worried and not so sad, except when she talked about Aunt Edna."

"That is sad. Believe me, when I write to Edna she's going to know what I think—what I know— she's missing by disowning her daughter. Say, isn't it about time for that boy to come? Aren't you going to change your clothes?"

"Yes, I've decided that this would be the right time to wear the pink dress. Maybe the older people

129

or the little ones like pretty colors—if they can see. What are you going to do while I'm gone?"

"I was getting ready to ask a favor of you. Could you run up to Louise's and see if she and Emilie would like to come over and share some cake and ice cream with me?"

After Mari was dressed she went outside and sat on the top step. *Some kids are playing ball somewhere close. I heard the crack of the bat before they began yelling.* A kite soared, then dipped in the soft blue sky.

The two little boys she'd seen before rode their tricycles on the sidewalk. One saw Mari and stopped so suddenly that the other bumped into him. "What you doing up there?"

"I live here."

"What's your name?"

"I'm Mari. Who are you?"

"I'm Mark. He's Scott. We're brothers."

"Hi, Mark and Scott. Want to come up?"

"We got to go. Our mama will worry about us."

"That's probably right. Good-bye." She watched the children pedal toward home. She glanced in the other direction and saw Kent Douglas coming toward her on the other side of the street. *Things sure look good,* she thought. *From where we are now they seem absolutely great.*

Dorothy Hamilton, a Selma, Indiana, housewife began writing books after she became a grandmother. As a private tutor, she has helped several hundred students with learning difficulties. Many of her books reflect the hurts she observed in her students. She offers hope to others in similar circumstances.

Mindy is caught in the middle of her parent's divorce. *Charco* and his family live on unemployment checks. *Jason* would like to attend a trade school, but his parents want him to go to college.

Other titles include: *Anita's Choice* (migrant workers), *Bittersweet Days* (snobbery at school), *The Blue Caboose* (less expensive housing), *Busboys at Big Bend* (Mexican-American friendship), *The Castle* (friendship), *Christmas for Holly* (a foster child), *Cricket* (a pony story), and *The Gift of a Home* (problems of becoming rich).

Mrs. Hamilton is also author of *Jim Musco* (a Delaware Indian boy), *Kerry* (growing up), *Linda's Rain Tree* (a black girl), *Mari's Mountain* (a runaway girl), *Neva's Patchwork Pillow* (Appalachia), *Rosalie* (life in grandma's day), *Straight Mark* (drugs), *Tony Savala* (a Basque boy), and *Winter Girl* (jealousy).

In addition to writing, Mrs. Hamilton has spoken to more than 1,200 groups of children in Indiana, Ontario, Pennsylvania, Tennessee, and Virginia, mostly in public schools.

"What's your favorite part in writing a book?" one young student asked.

"Right now, it's being here with you," she replied.

"The prospect of facing 80 fifth-and-sixth-graders at the same time is enough to send many adults for the nearest exit," a news reporter noted, "but for Dorothy Hamilton it is pure delight."